The Casebook of Private Investigator Sam Sloane

Stephen Towers

Copyright © 2024 Stephen Towers

All rights reserved.

ISBN:9798322779964

To my sister Sharman

To my sister Sharman

CONTENTS

Introduction

1. The Pharoah's Stone — Page 5
2. The School Charter — Page 77
3. A Gambling Problem — Page 139
4. Mind Games — Page 207
5. A Toxic Spa — Page 267
6. About the Author — Page 335

Once again I am deeply indebted to my good friend Keith Wilkinson and to my wife Judith for assisting me during the preparation of this book.

Thank you both for your time, patience and many suggestions, I sincerely appreciate it.

Introduction.

Originally an eighteenth-century coaching inn, the *Badger and Carrot* pub now stood sandwiched between a phone shop and a Turkish barber. Sam, who was a regular visitor to the pub, stood at the old timber-panelled bar waiting to be served. Moments later the landlord, Dave, appeared through the multi-coloured plastic strip door which separated the bar from his storeroom.

"Hello there, how are you keeping?" Dave said, smiling.

"I am good, thank you," Sam replied. "How are you?"

"Oh, can't complain. Pint of Old Peculier, is it?"

"Yes please."

This was the full extent of their conversation and had been for several years, other than the time Dave had emerged from his back room wearing an eyepatch - the result, he said, of an incident involving a non-English speaking Chinese tourist and an overly tight-fitting bra strap.

Dave never looked to be in good health, he frequently appeared to be sweating heavily and walked in a way which suggested he had just had a hip replacement. Which he hadn't, it was just that his stomach was so distended that it swayed when he walked and this affected his centre of gravity.

Sam liked the *Badger and Carrot*. There was no large-screen tv on the wall, no loud indistinguishable music playing, and it wasn't so popular that you couldn't hear yourself think. In Sam's opinion it was a "proper pub" where you could enjoy a pleasant drink after a day's work.

Sam sat down at a small table by the roaring fire. It wasn't that he was cold, it was because the only other vacant table was next to Sheila who, while sipping her pint of cider, was obviously deeply engrossed in studying the horse racing pages of her newspaper. Moreover, she unfortunately also suffered from halitosis and had a set of teeth which reminded Sam of a piano keyboard.

Sam reviewed the photographs he had taken an hour or so earlier. Clearly, he thought, the sacred vows of marriage aren't so sacred anymore and the pledge to love and honour your partner is as sincere as a politician's promise.

Sam took a drink of his beer, sat back in the well-worn leather seat and reflected. Although his aristocratic parents had made it abundantly clear that they were disappointed in their son's decision to become a private investigator - and to adopt the name "Sam Sloane" in place of his given name of "Bertram Edgeware", he had never regretted those decisions. As Sam saw it, he had been drawn to this type of work and for the moment at least could not see himself doing anything else. He smiled to himself and wondered what his next case might have in store for him.

Stephen Towers

The Casebook of Private Investigator Sam Sloane

The Pharoah's Stone

Stephen Towers

1.

It was early afternoon and Sam was at home with his feet up. Or, to be more precise, with one foot up. And that particular foot was attached to his right leg which was wrapped in a plaster cast and had been for three weeks.

The circumstances which had led to this situation were laughable now but not so much at the time. In a nutshell, Sam had been cycling to work when suddenly he had to swerve to avoid a small dog which had wandered onto the road. In performing this rarely practised manoeuvre Sam hit the kerb and fell from his bicycle. The dog owner, a rather large lady riding an equally large mobility scooter, having witnessed what had happened reversed her scooter to check Sam was not hurt. Unfortunately however, in doing so she accidently, some might say clumsily, ran over Sam's outstretched leg and broke it. To add insult to injury the lady's dog, which was on one of those extendable leads designed to irritate passers-by and cause accidents, then tried to hump Sam's good leg. Sam was neither amused nor receptive to the dog's advances. Later at the local hospital, when Sam described the incident to a young nurse in anticipation of some heartfelt sympathy, the nurse had to be led away by a colleague as she was at risk of having a seizure brought on by her uncontrollable laughter. So much for the caring profession, Sam had thought.

Initially the management and coordination of the plastered leg and use of the crutches proved not only inconvenient but also very problematic for Sam, who lacked the required coordination. He found himself not only sustaining additional injuries as a result, but frequently cursing the person who had invented extendable dog leads, who Sam frequently referred to simply as the *bloody idiot*. Sam found that he was only able to placate himself by concocting different forms of torture for the *bloody idiot* to endure, his favourite being the roasting of the person responsible on a skewer over an open fire. Fortunately, a week after the accident his parents left England for an impromptu two-month inspection of southern and central Africa. As a result, their butler James, was available to assist Sam. This also had the effect of improving Sam's mental well-being.

Sam decided to make use of his convalescence, and since the arrival of James began spending much of his time learning to play the electric guitar.

Sam would sit in his armchair balancing his recently purchased stringed instrument in his lap. The guitar was wired to a large black speaker which sat on the floor next to him, and a metronome, considered by the music shop sales assistant to be an essential piece of equipment to the would-be rock star, was balanced on one arm of the chair. A beginners guide to playing the guitar was held open on a kitchen stool placed in front of the armchair and rested alongside his elevated broken leg.

James for his part busied himself about the house, cooking, tidying, and regularly turning the pages of the beginner's guide. Although James had naturally not shared this with Sam, he was not a fan of the guitar.

"Well James, I think it is about time I gave it another go," Sam said enthusiastically, switching on the speaker.

"Is that advisable so soon after a heavy meal sir?" James replied in a concerned tone, while straightening the room curtains.

Sam strummed the guitar several times.

"Doesn't that sound really speak to you James?"

"It certainly does sir," James replied, dusting a window sill, and then quickly added, "I think it best if I dry the pots I washed earlier sir. I wouldn't want to be a distraction to you," and disappeared into the kitchen, closing the door firmly behind him.

It was mid-afternoon when James brought Sam a cup of tea and a selection of biscuits. This caused a break in the practice session.

"You know what, James"?

"No sir."

"I really think I am getting the hang of this," Sam said.

"Indeed sir, although you may wish to rest your fingers a while or you could risk some permanent damage."

Just then the house doorbell rang.

"Is that the doorbell James?"

"It certainly gave that impression sir," James replied making his way to the front door.

Moments later James returned and announced,

"Lady Veronica Stainton, sir."

"Veronica, this is an unexpected surprise," Sam said, forcing a smile.

Unfortunately, other than being a potential source for human organs, most people would struggle to find anything positive to say about Veronica. The term "totally self-centred" appeared to have been invented with her in mind. She was one of Sam's many cousins and following the suspicious death of her brother, who it seemed had fallen from the battlements of their stately home and stabbed himself on the way down, she was the sole heir to the Stainton's vast fortune.

Aside from buying expensive cars and clothes, Veronica often appeared in the society pages, usually pictured attending an event with a movie star or famous footballer on one of her arms. Apart from being a manic self-publicist she also had a reputation for acting recklessly. It was rumoured that a traffic warden who had once given her a parking ticket woke up one morning to find her entire house and its contents painted yellow. It was also said that a postie who complained because he was bitten by her dog was drugged, secured in a wooden crate, and parcelled off to Alaska.

"How are you? And what are you doing here?" Sam asked, although not particularly interested in the former, but curious about the latter as they had not spoken since the last family funeral, which was when Sam tended to see his relatives.

"I have a job for you," she said bluntly.

"Oh," Sam replied, rather surprised.

"I understand you are a private investigator. Well, I have something for you to do which requires the utmost discretion."

"I am listening, but, and it may be a big but, you might have noticed I have a broken leg," Sam said.

"Oh, for goodness' sake, if you are going to be full of excuses, it is only a broken leg, it is not as if I am asking you for a kidney. Are you able to help me or not?" Veronica said, clearly irritated.

"Well, I don't know what it is you would like me to do, unfortunately I am not a mind reader," Sam said.

"Well, that is fortunate, because if you knew what I was thinking right now...." Veronica blurted.

"Would you like a cup of tea?" Sam interrupted trying to restore an air of calm.

"No, I would not like a cup of tea. What I would like is my photographs back."

"Your photographs?" Sam asked.

"Yes, Frankie Doyle, the owner of The Pyramid Club, has some photographs of me which could be rather embarrassing if they got out. In fact, the press would have a field day."

At that moment James entered the room carrying a small tray with two cups of tea and some Victoria sponge cake. Sam thought he saw James raise his eyebrows at over hearing Veronica's news.

"The Pyramid Club?" Sam asked Veronica.

"Yes, the Pyramid Club. It is the place where everyone who is anyone goes. It is the place to be seen. Don't you know it? For goodness' sake Bertie, what do you do for entertainment?" Veronica replied.

"Actually, I am currently learning to play the guitar, aren't I James?"

"Indeed sir," James replied, and left the room.

"It may seem the obvious thing to say, but I assume you have asked for these photographs?"

"Yes, of course, but he has refused to hand them over. He keeps them locked in his office desk at the club. He said he will only give them to me if I give him the Pharoah's Sapphire. I told him the stone is not mine to give, it is mummy's and it has been a family heirloom for generations and there is no way she would part with it. So, he said to tell him where it is so he could acquire it."

"Steal it?" Sam instinctively said.

"Gee, you think?" Veronica replied.

"You mustn't tell him," Sam said.

"Well, that is the second half of my problem. I told him mummy was taking it to a ball in Venice and she was travelling on the Orient Express. If she finds out what I have done I am sure it will be the last straw. My parents will probably disinherit me. You must get the photographs and stop him from stealing the Pharoah's Sapphire."

"Who is this, Frankie Doyle? Apart from being the owner of The Pyramid Club I mean?" Sam asked.

"He is a local gangland boss," Veronica casually replied.

"What?" Sam exclaimed.

"And he can be pretty mean, I don't mind telling you," Veronica said, "He once broke someone's fingers because he thought they had a small irritating moustache."

"Okay, I get the picture, there is no need for you to sugar-coat it. After all, trying to be positive for a moment, I suppose I already have one broken leg."

"So, you will do it?" Veronica said.

"I will look into it and get back to you. But I can't promise anything."

"Oh, thank you Bertie, I knew I could rely on you," and with that Veronica jumped up and rushed out of the house.

Moments later, having closed the house front door, James returned to where Sam was sitting.

"Tell me James, why is it there is never a mongoose around when you need one?"

"One of life's enduring mysteries, sir."

2.

A light rain was falling steadily. Although not wanting to attract any undue attention, two figures stood conspicuously beneath a street lamp. The taller of the two wore a dark suit, grey waistcoat, a tie and highly polished black shoes. He was holding a large black umbrella and sheltering the other man, who was dressed in a raincoat and trilby and had a plaster cast on his right leg.

"You couldn't describe them as being big on advertising, could you James?"

"No, sir."

On the opposite side of the narrow street was The Pyramid Club. It was almost indistinguishable from the other buildings in that street: no neon lights, no loud music coming from within, no queues of people waiting to enter. There was a simple small brass name plaque, in front of which stood two very well-dressed, remarkedly big men. Their outward demeanour was such that you would not have been surprised to learn that they had been hounded from their homes by villagers wielding burning torches and pitch forks.

Turning to James, Sam said,

"This might prove tricky."

"Indeed sir, and although I readily recognise that first impressions can be misleading, and it is often said that one should not judge a book by its cover, I cannot help but get the distinct impression of a strong undercurrent of mindless violence from within the establishment."

"Thank you for sharing that, James."

"Not at all, sir."

"Any suggestions?" Sam asked.

"Well as the photographs you are seeking are understood to be in Mr Doyle's desk, and if as I assume he would be indisposed to give them to you, I would suggest that in order to facilitate your recovery of the said images, we need to ensure Mr Doyle is distracted in some way. Ideally, not on the premises when you facilitate your entry."

"Okay, with you so far James, but how?"

"Well sir, I understand that Mr Doyle has a fascination for Egyptian antiquities. Possibly a telephonic communication advising him of the sudden and immediate availability of such an antiquity, for example, a small ivory statue of King Khufu, the second pharaoh of the fourth dynasty, may suffice to initiate his speedy departure from the club?"

"Good idea, James. As you seem to have a certain knowledge of these things would you make the call?"

"Certainly sir. I have taken the liberty of keying in the number in readiness."

Less than ten minutes later, a large black car stopped outside The Pyramid Club. One of the two big men standing at the entrance door took out his mobile phone and made a call. Moments later the door to the club opened and out hurried a small rotund man wearing a heavy coat with a large fur collar. The door to the car was opened for him, he got in and the car sped off with a screech of wheels splashing water from the puddles onto the pavement.

"Well, if that was Frankie Doyle getting into the car, which I guess it was, then your phone call certainly had the desired effect, James."

"I took the further liberty sir, of advising that another interested party was already en route with a view to purchasing the statue. This seems to have stimulated his ambition."

"I'll say. Anyway, no time like the present. Wish me luck James."

"Good luck, sir."

With his crutch firmly placed under his right arm, Sam crossed the street toward the club's entrance door and the two men standing in front of it. As he got nearer, he was able to hear their conversation.

"So, your argument is Einstein's theory is basically flawed because you believe it is not about the speed of light, rather it is about the density of the space through which the light travels."

"Correct, and as a result we need to shift our focus on to the folding or collapsing of space in order to traverse it more quickly,"

"And you believe molecular fusion rather than dispiration is the answer?"

"If we use digital titanium plates and heavy ion confinement with a multi-beam particle accelerator. Otherwise, you risk setting off a negative chain reaction."

"Yes, I get that."

As Sam approached their conversation stopped and they turned their attention to him.

"What do you want?" one of them said in an accusing tone.

"I would like to go into the club please," Sam replied.

"Are you a member?"

"No," Sam said.

"Are you on the guest list?"

"I don't suppose so."

"Then sod off or we will break your other leg."

"Come on, why not? It looks a nice place," Sam pleaded.

"Do you know this establishment is regularly visited by movie stars, footballers, members of the royal family, and such like."

"No, I didn't know that. But I would still like to go in please," Sam said.

"What really?" one of the big men said, in a disbelieving tone.

"Yes, really."

"Fair enough, in you go," and he opened one of the entrance doors for Sam to enter.

Once through the door Sam found himself in a sizeable lobby. The walls were decorated in hieroglyphics and ancient Egyptian artwork. The ceiling was a dark blue colour embellished with numerous stars. At one end of the room stood a pair of artificial life size palm trees and next to these was a counter where club visitors could leave their coats. Behind the counter was a young woman dressed in a white wraparound gown, a gold coloured nemes headdress, sandals, and various heavy jewellery.

"May I take your hat and coat?" she asked Sam.

"Yes please," Sam replied and then indicating toward a pair of doors he asked, "This is my first time here, is that the way into the club?"

"Yes, it is," she said, smiling.

Sam however was more interested in the staircase he had seen beyond another door which had been left slightly ajar, possibly by a person in a great hurry, and as soon as the young woman turned her back to hang up his coat, Sam slipped through that door as quickly as a person with a broken leg could.

Ascending a narrow stairway using a crutch and dragging a leg in plaster is not as easy as a lot of people might think. More so when you are trying to do it without attracting the attention of others. Eventually after no small effort, a heavy breathing Sam reached the top and a single door marked "Private".

As quietly as he could, he put his ear to the door and listened. He could hear nothing from within. Now, in an effort to make as little sound as possible, while holding his breath he slowly turned the door handle and gently opened the door. Peeping inside he thankfully found that no one was in the room.

As quickly as he could he hopped over to the large desk which stood in the middle of the room. Then, putting his weight on the desk with one hand he leaned his crutch against the side of the desk and with his now free hand tried the desk drawers. To his disappointment he found that they were all locked. There was a letter opener on the desk and Sam tried this to force the drawer, but unfortunately only succeeded in bending it, and the drawers remained locked. Just then Sam's mobile phone rang, it was James.

"Good evening, sir, I do apologise for interrupting whatever you are doing at this moment, but I thought it best to advise you that Mr Doyle has just returned to the club."

"Okay, thank you James, must dash, bye."

"Goodbye, sir."

Moments later, as Sam was making his way as quickly as he could to the office door, he heard an angry voice on the other side of it.

"If I ever find out who sent me on that wild goose chase, they will regret being born. I will pull out their organs and mummify them. Statue of King Khufu my eye."

The office door swung open and Sam stood face to face with Frankie Doyle.

"Who the hell are you and what are you doing in my office?"

3.

"Now that is a very good question, one which deserves a very good answer," Sam said. "In fact, if I were in your shoes, I too would be wondering what was going on. Well, let me tell you. I say that but I don't mean to be presumptuous. I mean I don't want to be taking up your valuable time, as I am sure you probably have lots of better things to do than listen to me. Do you think it is a bit cold out tonight? That is a very nice coat you are wearing. I bet it is nice and warm. Is it?"

Frankie Doyle stared menacingly up at Sam,

"You are running out of time and I am running out of patience."

"Well, it's like this Mr Doyle. May I call you that? This is my first time in your wonderful club and I thought this might be the customer's toilet."

Frankie turned to the very big man who was standing silently and expressionless behind him and said,

"I am just not having a very good day, am I? Gag and tie him George, and put him in the store room until I decide what to do with him."

Before Sam could say "Hold on!" George had grabbed him by the collar of his jacket and Sam was being led down the stairs, which was probably a good thing, because on his way down he heard Frankie shout,

"What have you done to my letter opener? My mother gave me that."

Although Sam did not consider himself any sort of an authority on store rooms, the one he had been roughly bundled into seemed the same as any other he imagined, apart from the dried pools of blood on the floor. As he looked about, he could see boxes of supermarket wine, no doubt, he guessed, sold at a massive mark-up, some stacked tables and chairs, a roll of piano wire, and a collection of DIY tools.

It was cold and damp. Sam wondered if his cousin Veronica was upstairs right now having a good time, possibly chatting to a movie star or a member of the royal family. He had failed in his attempt to retrieve the photographs she eagerly sought and he felt bad about that, but then what was she thinking about in the first place? He was in this predicament because of her lack of judgement. He looked at the piano wire and the collection of tools which like the floor of the storeroom also appeared to be blood stained. Was he soon to experience the persuasive effect of a pneumatic nail gun or a pair of needle nose pliers? Rather than wait to find out the answer he decided to focus his energies on escaping as fast as he could.

The heavy-duty cable ties which held his hands and feet were tightly bound. Not only that, his plastered leg was also restricting his movement and he was struggling to stand up. He rolled across the dusty floor toward the tool box passing what at first glance appeared to be a severed finger. He decided not to give it a second glance. He could see a small hacksaw which he thought he could use to cut his ties. Unfortunately, however, despite painfully contorting himself in ways which to the best of his recollection he hadn't done before, and despite an increased amount of cursing which included reference to the inventor of extendable dog leads, Sam was unable to hold the saw in a way which he could employ it to cut his ties. Exhausted from his efforts he fell back, hitting his head on a table leg. In doing so however, he noticed what appeared to be a broken exotic dancer's pole in the corner of the store. Although not something he was accustomed to doing, he rolled up close to it and noticed the chrome pole had a sharp edge where it was damaged, possibly by an overweight pole dancer, or one who got a little carried away somehow. Rubbing his hand ties against the sharp edge he found he was able to cut the ties. Within minutes Sam was free of his shackles.

With renewed energy Sam managed to pick up his crutch and crossed to the storeroom door, but only to find not surprisingly, that the heavy door was bolted from the outside. Although not a DIY enthusiast himself, in fact Sam tended to refer to the initialism as Destroy It Yourself, he made his way back to the tools to see if there was anything he could use to open the room door. As he did so his mobile phone, which his captors had not thought to take, made a sound which told him that someone had left him a message. On the off chance that it was not a spam message or someone trying to sell him a more efficient boiler, he thought he would check it.

"Hello Mr Sloane, it's Barbara, your secretary. I just thought you should know. Well, I wasn't sure if you would want to know so I wasn't going to mention it, but then I changed my mind and thought I would tell you because I thought you might want to know. A woman called to our office today and got very annoyed that you were not here. I told her you weren't in but she thought that you should be. She said she was a relative of yours but I told her that I knew she couldn't be because she wasn't a very nice person. She said she didn't care what I thought and called me a simpleton who had obviously just crawled out of the ocean and never evolved any further. I told her that couldn't be me because I don't like swimming. Anyway, she said she knew where you lived and was going to your house. I think she said her name was Victoria, or was it Venetia? It could have been Sarah, no when I think about it, it wasn't Sarah, that was the woman I met in the queue in the butcher's this morning, or was that yesterday? Hope your leg is better. By the way if you don't need this message don't listen to it. Bye."

Sam took a moment to simply raise his eyebrows, then he put his phone back into his jacket pocket and looked down at the tools. Unfortunately, nothing obvious presented itself. He sat himself down on one of the plastic wrapped chairs and stared at the room door waiting for inspiration to strike and bring with it a good idea as to how he may escape. After a short while Sam took out his mobile phone.

"Hello James, it's me."

"Good evening, sir, I hope all goes well with your mission."

"Sadly, not as well as I had hoped James."

"I am distressed to hear that, sir. May I be of any assistance?"

"Well, this is the situation. Although I found Frankie Doyle's office, I was unable to retrieve the photographs my cousin wants. Worse still, I have been locked in a storeroom, and am awaiting imminent interrogation. Right now, any thoughts you may have would be most welcome."

"Leave it with me sir."

Dumbfounded, Sam returned his mobile phone to his jacket pocket and looking about the room wondered what James had in mind.

After about ten minutes Sam heard the sound of much commotion outside the storeroom door, he also noticed that he was becoming increasingly wet. He then heard the distinctive noise of a fire alarm. Was this James plan or was it a genuine fire? he thought. Sam made his way to the room door and began banging on it with his crutch, hoping that at the very least a passer-by would hear him and open the door. Several minutes passed and the door suddenly opened.

"Good evening, sir. May I ask you to follow me please."

"Certainly James, please lead on," a surprised, damp looking Sam said.

Passing several firemen running into the club, Sam and James made their way out of the building and got into a passing taxi.

"Thank you for that James, much appreciated."

"You are most welcome, sir."

"Shame we didn't manage to get those photographs, I know my cousin Veronica will not be best pleased."

"Not wanting to contradict you sir, but I have the said photographs here." James pulled a brown envelope from his inside jacket pocket and handed it to Sam.

Sam peered inside the envelope, which contained a memory stick and some A4 prints, which he quickly resolved never to unfold. He sealed the envelope.

"Oh, that's fantastic, but how did you manage that?" Sam asked.

"Well sir, although it embarrasses me to say so, before I released you from the storeroom, I saw Mr Doyle hastily leaving the building and so I took the opportunity to make my way to his office and removed the items."

"So, there wasn't an actual fire then?" Sam asked.

"No sir. it seems the fire system was activated when someone presented a naked flame to one of the fire detectors."

"You did that?" Sam said, in a surprised voice.

"I really couldn't say, sir."

4.

The next day dawned and as Sam began to stir the door to his bedroom silently opened.

"Good morning, sir, I hope you slept well," James said, carrying a large wooden bed tray. "I have brought your breakfast, two boiled eggs, four rashers of lean bacon, lightly buttered toast, yogurt, and coffee."

"Thank you, James, just what I need having managed to escape the questionable hospitality of the Pyramid Club," Sam said, pulling himself up and adjusting his pillows to create a comfortable sitting position in his bed. "How is the weather out there today?"

"Extremely clement, sir, there is a gentle south-south-westerly breeze, some cumulus humilis clouds are in evidence in an otherwise blue sky, and there is a forecast maximum temperature of nineteen degrees Celsius," James replied, while opening the room curtains and then neatly folding Sam's clothes on to a nearby chair.

"A good day to let my cousin Veronica know that we have managed to recover her photographs."

"Indeed, sir, shall there be anything else?"

"No thank you, James."

Once washed and ready Sam rang his cousin.

"Good morning, Veronica, it's Bertie, I thought that you would like to know that I have your photographs," he said pleasingly.

"Fine, I will be at your house within the hour to collect them," she replied, and with that the phone connection and any chance of conversation was ended.

"You are welcome," Sam said to himself and put his phone down.

Sam made his way through to his kitchen where James was washing some dishes.

"There really is no need for you to wash up James, I am perfectly capable of doing so."

"Thank you, sir, but if it is all the same to you I would rather do it."

"As you choose. By the way my cousin Veronica will be coming around in the next hour or so to collect her photographs."

"Very well, sir. Would you like me to prepare anything in particular in readiness for her visit?"

"Other than the odd booby trap, I shouldn't bother."

"Just as you say, sir."

It was shortly after lunch when the front doorbell rang. James opened the door and without a word Veronica brushed passed him.

"Good afternoon, miss," James said. There was no response.

Veronica entered the living room to find Sam examining the metronome he had bought on the shop assistant's recommendation.

"What's that you are playing with?" she asked.

"Hello Veronica, it's called a metronome."

"Really, sounds fascinating," she said sarcastically. "Do you have my photos?"

"Here they are," Sam replied handing them to her. "We expected you earlier."

"Well, I do have a life, you know. Which reminds me, I need you to run an errand for me. I need you to go down to the local registry office."

"What on earth for?" Sam asked.

"I am supposed to be getting married there at 4.00pm. You need to tell the groom that I have changed my mind."

"You have got to be kidding," Sam replied incredulously.

"No, and stop being so dramatic, it doesn't suit you. His name is John Ramshaw. And don't forget you have got to prevent Frankie Doyle getting his dirty fingers on the Pharoah's Sapphire. Mummy will be most upset if he steals it. Anyway, must dash, I am off to Monaco to a charity ball."

"Which charity?" Sam asked out of interest.

"No idea," Veronica replied and promptly left.

When James returned to the living room Sam asked him,

"What is wrong with my cousin?"

"I really couldn't say sir. Rumour has it when she was born the midwife cried uncontrollably, church walls ran with blood and dogs howled and formed into packs."

"Sadly, I can believe all that," Sam replied.

"Now what am I going to do about this John Ramshaw? The poor chap is going to be left at the altar as it were. It is the sort of thing that could scar a person for life. I am going to have to see him, I can't just let him stand there waiting for a person who we know has no intention of turning up. What do I say? Talk about terrible news."

"Rather I imagine, like announcing the start of yet another celebrity game show on television, sir."

"Indeed James, well, almost as bad as that," Sam replied reflectively.

....

"The Registrar's Office please," Sam told the taxi driver.

"Oh, big day, is it? You getting married? I remember when I got married. Almost thirty years ago now. Best looking girl around, I thought," the taxi driver said and seemingly floated off for a moment with his fond memories. Then he returned, "She looks very different now. So big she almost blocks out the sun. Dare not go into a cake or a sweet shop, she just breaks out in a cold sweat. She fell over once and landed on our dog. Killed it outright she did. I loved that dog."

"No, I am not getting married," Sam replied trying to return the taxi driver's concentration to the traffic.

"Best man, are you?"

"Afraid not, no," Sam replied.

"Great institution marriage. But you have to work at it. Did you know nearly half of all marriages in this country end in divorce? Personally, I blame the Russians. You can't trust a Russian. Any way here we are mate. That will be eight quid. Mind my paintwork as you get out with that crutch."

Sam paid the driver and struggled out of the taxi.

The Registrar's Office was accommodated in a small single storey building. There were surprisingly few windows and those that there were had metal frames and frosted glass. Like the Pyramid Club, the service was not big on advertising, the only indication of its presence being a small brass plaque next to the blue entrance door, which was in need of some oil. Sam opened the door to a loud squeak and entered a small reception area.

"Good afternoon, how may I help you?" asked an elderly looking man, sitting behind an equally elderly looking desk.

"Hello, I am looking for John Ramshaw. I understand he is supposed to be getting married here at four o clock," Sam replied.

"Supposed to be?" the elderly man said curiously.

"Yes, I am afraid I have some bad news for him," Sam said very soberly.

"Oh, that is unfortunate. He is through there in the waiting room," the man said pointing to another door.

Sam opened the waiting room door to a much bigger room which was simply but pleasantly decorated. It had a heavy carpet and a large chandelier hung from the ceiling. Several well-dressed people wearing flowers stood around. They all turned to see who had just entered and smiled politely when they saw Sam.

"I am looking for a John Ramshaw," Sam said in a tone which suggested he was about to impart bad news.

A tall, slim man in a light grey suit stood forward,

"I am John Ramshaw, what can I do for you?" he asked in a serious tone.

"I am not sure if there is a right way of saying this, but I am afraid I have some bad news for you. I am sorry to have to tell you that Veronica has had a change of heart and has decided not to get married."

"What?" John said, "she doesn't want to get married?"

"That's right, I am very sorry," Sam replied.

Slowly but surely, John began to smile and then shouted,

"That's great. That's brilliant. I was drunk when I proposed to her and later wished I hadn't but didn't want to hurt her. This is fantastic news," John said and gave Sam a big hug and announced, "Let's all go to the pub and get hammered."

The elderly man in the reception was obviously surprised when the groom, his best man, and the witnesses left singing, shouting and dancing.

"I thought you said you had some bad news for him?" he said to Sam who was following everyone out with his crutch under his arm.

"So did I," Sam replied, and shrugged his shoulders.

"You don't happen to have any bad news for me, do you?" the man asked hopefully.

"Afraid not, sorry."

As requested, Sam joined the rest of the wedding party in The Fox and Hounds pub, which was a few doors down from the Registrar's office. As it turned out John Ramshaw, besides being an honourable person, and now a much relieved one, was a professional footballer. He had met Veronica at the Pyramid Club one evening after he had scored a hat trick for his country and so was out celebrating. Egged on by some of his team mates, clearly he had taken the celebrations a bit too far.

Later that day while on his way home Sam smiled to himself. He recalled how much he had felt sorry for John Ramshaw being abandoned at the registry office. How Sam had not been looking forward to breaking the news to him, and how John had celebrated upon hearing the news. It's funny how things sometimes turn out. And clearly there are still some principled people in this world, he thought.

"That will be ten quid," the driver said when the taxi pulled up outside Sam's home.

"But I only paid eight quid a few hours ago for the same journey," Sam protested.

Needless to say, Sam, suddenly brought back down to earth, didn't give a tip.

5.

"Good evening, sir. I hope your visit to the Registrar's Office went as well as could be expected," James said as Sam entered his front door.

"Much better than expected actually. As it turned out, John Ramshaw was delighted not to be marrying my cousin. In fact, I have just come from the pub where they are still celebrating."

"That is indeed good news, sir."

"Isn't it James. Frankly, in my opinion, Mr Ramshaw doesn't know how lucky he is to have dodged that particular bullet."

"As you say, sir. On a related matter, while you were out there was a telephonic communication from Lord and Lady Stainton. It seems that their daughter, Veronica happened to mention to them that she had recently seen you, and they thought as they had not had the pleasure of your company for some time, you may care to visit them in the near future."

"Well James, under normal circumstances I would be content to limit my contact with my aunt and uncle, harmless as they are, to a snow scene Christmas card. However, as there is still the small matter of the security of the Pharoah's Sapphire, maybe it would be an opportune time to call upon them. Book a couple of train tickets if you would James, and we will go tomorrow."

"Very good, sir."

………………..

"Harmless" was a word often used to describe Lord and Lady Stainton. So were "kind hearted, gullible, and dumb." On one occasion, on an unaccompanied visit to the local village High Street, they had purchased an area of Antarctica from someone they recalled as "a very pleasant young man." The man, who they believed they had accidently but fortuitously bumped in to, had expressed great concern regarding the penguins, which he believed would soon become extinct, unless some kind hearted person or persons stepped in to help. As luck would have it, he also happened to have in his jacket pocket the deeds to a large part of Antarctica which he had inherited as a child, but unfortunately now had to sell in order to pay for his ailing grandmother's much needed operation. As always Lord and Lady Stainton were eager to assist. Although at the last moment the purchase almost fell through when Lady Stainton perceptively queried why the printed address on their receipt was that of the local betting shop. The young man was however quick to reassure them that Vegas Gaming was in fact the new name for Antarctica. The name having to be changed for tax reasons. "Seems reasonable enough to me," Lord Stainton had been heard to comment. He and his wife were always inclined to think the best of people, and to help where they could. Needless to say, people often wondered if Veronica was in fact their biological daughter.

....

The gravel drive lightly crunched under the tyres of the black taxi as it came to a gentle halt outside the grand front door of Croxley Manor, the residence of the Stainton family for generations.

With his plastered leg uncomfortably outstretched, Sam edged his way along the back seat of the taxi and out of the car door which James held open. Then, with the aid of his crutch, the door and James, he pulled himself to his feet.

"Thank you, James. I think I am starting to get the hang of this."

"I am delighted to hear that sir," James replied.

As the taxi pulled away a voice behind Sam shouted,

"Bertie, how nice to see you. But what have you done to your leg?"

Sam turned to see his aunt and uncle followed by their butler, Chilvers, who was carrying an empty metal bucket.

"Hello there," Sam replied smiling broadly, and pointing to his broken leg said dismissively, "This? Oh, I just had a small accident. It is nothing really. Looks worse than it is," but felt his blood pressure rise as he said so, and calmed himself by picturing a certain inventor hanging from a lamppost with an arrow through their neck.

"Looks jolly uncomfortable to me, young Bertie," Lady Stainton replied.

"Erm, forgive me for asking," Sam said, "probably none of my business. But why are you both dressed as giant penguins?"

"Oh, we have been feeding the birds," Lord Stainton replied.

"The birds?" Sam replied a little mystified.

"The penguins. We try to make them feel at home so we wear these outfits when we feed them their fish."

"Oh, I see," Sam said, unconvincingly.

"Shall we go inside and have some tea?" Lady Stainton suggested.

"I would love a cup, thank you," Sam replied. And they all went inside where Lord and Lady Stainton removed their penguin costumes to reveal matching outfits of tweed plus four trousers, waistcoats and jackets. For some reason which no one cared to ask, they always dressed the same on Thursdays.

A roaring fire burned in the inglenook fireplace of the drawing room. Sam, his aunt and uncle sat in large armchairs around a large marble coffee table. After about twenty minutes, Chilvers and James entered the room and served tea and an assortment of finger sandwiches, scones and petit fours.

"What a coincidence you bumping into Veronica," Lady Stainton said.

"Wasn't it," Sam replied.

"She is such a sensitive girl, we do worry about her at times, afraid someone may take advantage of her good nature."

"Veronica?" Sam said, somewhat astounded and wondered if she maybe had an identical twin he had never met.

"If only she could meet someone who could look after her, guide her through life, as it were," Lady Stainton said in an anxious voice.

Then Lord Stainton turned to his nephew and with a very serious expression said,

"I don't know if your parents have mentioned anything to you Bertie, but we were wondering if you would like to marry her?"

"Me!" Sam exclaimed.

"Well, we thought you would be ideal for her. Your parents seem comfortable with the idea."

"Oh, they do, do they?" Sam said, still in a state of shock. Turning to James who was pouring tea Sam said frantically grasping at straws, "Isn't it illegal to marry one's cousin James?"

"Not in the United Kingdom, sir."

"Oh, is that right, thank you, James," Sam replied grimacing.

"There is however the matter of your genetic disorder which as you have selflessly indicated previously, you would not wish to pass on to another. And scientific research has confirmed the greater likelihood of doing so if one married a blood relative," James said.

"Yes, of course, there is that," Sam said, wondering what on earth James was referring to, but nevertheless happy to play along. Sam shook his head as if dismayed and burdened by his problem which he had consciously decided to bear alone.

"Your parents never mentioned that," Lord Stainton said in both a surprised and concerned tone.

"We don't like to talk about it," Sam added in order to close the conversation topic off.

"Shame, but there you go," Lady Stainton said taking a drink of tea. "Veronica tells us you are a private eye. That sounds exciting."

"It has its moments," Sam said, smiling.

"Are you working on anything interesting at the moment?" Lady Stainton asked.

"Actually, I am trying to prevent a jewel robbery."

"How fascinating. It's not the crown jewels, is it?" Lord Stainton said laughing.

"I understand the jewel involved did once belong to the Egyptian monarchy," Sam replied hoping his aunt and uncle would make the connection. He didn't want to shock the innocent pair by being direct.

"So, it must be an old stone then. Where is it going to be stolen from?"

"I believe the thieves are going to try and steal it from the owners when they are travelling on board the Orient Express," Sam said, again hoping his relatives would fill in the blanks.

"Well, bugger me with a fish fork, we are travelling on the Orient Express soon ourselves. Off to a ball in Venice. Nice place, well if you like water. Lots of rats I have heard. Water rats I suspect. Saw one once. My word, the size of it. An enormous black thing. It was so big there was a man riding on its back," Sam's uncle said, clearly having drifted off topic.

"That was a gondola dear," Lady Stainton said kindly to her husband.

"Was it? Mind you, I did wonder why the man on its back was wearing a straw hat and singing," her husband replied.

"If you recall that was the day you forgot to take your medication, and you drank rather a lot of Grappa brandy."

"I didn't forget to take my medication; the pharmacist sent my medicine to the wrong address."

"You gave them the wrong address," Lady Stainton replied in a kind, caring tone.

"Impossible, how could I forget where I was staying? It is like saying I would forget that I live here at…."

"Croxley Hall, dear."

"I knew that. I was just thinking about it for a moment," Lord Stainton replied defensively.

"So, you are going to a ball in Venice?" Sam asked trying to move the conversation along.

"Yes, a week on Wednesday. We are looking forward to it. I am going to wear the Pharoah's Sapphire," Lady Stainton said.

"Really? I have never seen that stone," Sam said.

"Oh, it is beautiful, Chilvers would you fetch the Pharoah's Sapphire for Bertram to see please."

"Certainly madam."

A short time later Chilvers returned with a small green velvet box which he handed to Lady Stainton, who in turn passed it to her nephew. Sam opened the box.

"My word, I don't think I have ever seen anything like it. I hope you have it insured," he said laughing.

"Oh yes, we would hate to lose it. The story is the stone was found in the belly of a crocodile shot on the Nile. Probably in the pocket of some poor unsuspecting fellow who went down for a refreshing early morning dip and became breakfast. Been in the family for years. Here Chilvers, better put it back in the safe," Lady Stainton handed Chilvers the box with the stone in it and Chilvers and James left the drawing room.

"I say Bertie, you don't think anyone will try and steal the Pharoah's Sapphire, do you?" Lord Stainton asked.

"Well, it is a very valuable stone. If you are taking it with you, I should take great care of it," Sam replied, trying not to worry his kindly relatives but at the same time conscious that

Veronica had told him in confidence that there was a good chance Frankie Doyle would try and get his hands on it.

"We will Bertie, thank you for the advice. Another sandwich?"

………………..

The train journey home was an unusually quiet one. The carriage where Sam and James sat was almost empty, and those few passengers who were there were not the worse for drink, nor did they feel the need to talk loudly into their mobile phones. Sam sat looking out of the window deep in thought. James sat silently reading his book, "Sir Isaac Newton's Mathematical Principles". Then suddenly Sam turned to James and said,

"James, we have no other option, we have to be on that train to Venice."

"Just as you say, sir," James calmly replied.

6.

"Bonjour Messieurs, welcome to the Orient Express. May I see your tickets please?" a tall, slightly built man in a bright blue gold braided uniform said.

James handed over the tickets which the tall man gratefully received in his lily-white gloves.

"Ah, yes, please follow me. My name is Claude and it is my pleasure to serve you on our journey to Venice. Should you need anything or have any queries please do not hesitate to ask me."

Having been escorted to their wood-panelled cabin, Sam turned to Claude and said,

"I believe two of my relatives, Lord and Lady Stainton, are also travelling on this train. Would you please advise them that their nephew is on board, should they wish to meet for a drink or something to eat."

"Certainly, sir," Claude replied giving a well-practised smile, and then disappeared down the carriage corridor.

It wasn't long before the train, made famous through the Agatha Christie novel, gently moved off and left the station on its journey. A short while later there was a knock on Sam's cabin door. It was Claude.

"Sorry to disturb you, sir. I hope everything is to your satisfaction?" but before Sam was able to respond he continued, "Lord and Lady Stainton have suggested you meet in Bar Car 3674 at 10.00am for tea."

"Excellent, thank you, Claude," Sam replied, and closed his cabin door.

"This is certainly some train isn't it, James. Probably the most famous train in the world I imagine. I wonder how it all started?" Sam mused.

"It was the brainchild of the Belgian engineer Georges Nagelmackers, who in 1865 envisioned a train that would span a continent running on a continuous ribbon of metal for more than 1,500 miles. Nagelmackers was the son of a banker…"

"Right, thank you James, I think that is probably enough locomotive information for now," Sam interrupted.

"As you say, sir."

Sam sat quietly gazing out of the window at the passing landscape. James unpacked the overnight bags and neatly arranged the clothes in the limited hanging space available. After a short while Sam checked his watch and, finding it was approaching 10.00am, he stood up.

"Well, James, I think it is about time we made our way to the refreshments car and see what my dear relatives have been up to. And check on the whereabouts of the Pharoah's Sapphire."

"Indeed sir," James replied and instinctively began brushing Sam's jacket.

"Just leave it James, the jacket is fine."

"It is important for a gentleman to be smartly presented at all times, sir," James replied.

"Very well, okay that's enough, let's go," and Sam and James made their way to Bar Car

3674, where they found Lord and Lady Stainton already seated.

"Good morning," Sam said.

"Good morning to you, Bertram. What a pleasant coincidence to find that you should be travelling on the same train as ourselves. It must be a morning for coincidences. Why just a few moments ago your aunt and I were chatting to a man who said he too was going to Venice."

"Really," Sam said, totally unsurprised.

"Not only that, he said he was a mind reader. He said, now stay with me here Bertie, he said, I bet you are carrying a very valuable stone. And when I said we were, he said, and I bet it has an Egyptian history. Well of course it has, it is the Pharoah's Sapphire which your aunt intends to wear at the charity ball tomorrow night. Well, I don't mind telling you your aunt and I were amazed. Isn't that amazing?"

"It certainly is. Isn't that amazing James?"

"Most illuminating sir."

"Tell me uncle," Sam said, "What did this man look like?"

"Well, if asked to describe him I would say he was a man of below average height, who would probably benefit from losing a few pounds. He wore a heavy looking coat with a large fur collar. Pleasant chap."

Sam glanced at James who said nothing but simply lifted his eyebrows.

"I say Bertie, you don't think this mind reading fellow could be the jewel thief you are searching for?" Lord Stainton said, in a surprised tone.

"Well, to the best of my knowledge no robbery has actually taken place so far, but I still have reason to believe that it may well take place on this train journey. I am trying to prevent the robbery."

"Oh, I don't think I will be able to relax until we are in Venice," Lady Stainton said in a concerned voice.

"If it would make you feel any better, I will look after the Pharoah's Sapphire until we get to Venice," Sam said.

"Oh, would you Bertram," his aunt replied in a calmer voice. "I would appreciate that."

"Dearest aunt, I would be more than happy to oblige. Where do you have it?"

"It's in our compartment."

"Well, as soon as we have finished our tea, James will accompany you to your compartment and relieve you of your stone. Then I will return it to you when we arrive in Venice, and you can wear it at your ball for everyone to see.

....

"Ah James, you are back," Sam said as his travelling companion entered their cabin.

"Yes, sir."

"Did you get the stone?"

"Yes, sir. Lady Stainton also gave me these custard cream biscuits for you sir. She recalled you enjoyed them as a child."

"Did I?"

"Apparently, sir. She also recalled you particularly enjoyed green jelly, but neglected to pack any."

"Green jelly? Sounds disgusting."

"Yes, sir."

"Okay, where are we going to hide this jewel?" Sam asked.

"Well, sir. Conscious that the cabin is transformed by the carriage steward into sleeping quarters this evening, I would suggest that you keep the jewel about your person until after that event."

"Good idea, James."

"Thank you, sir."

…..……………

It was early evening when Sam and James made their way to the train's dining car. Then after a restorative cocktail at the bar they were shown to their reserved table, only to discover that sitting at another table within a Danish pastry throwing distance, was Frankie Doyle.

Soon after they had sat down Sam and James were joined by Lord and Lady Stainton.

"That's him, that's that mind reading fellow I was telling you about," Lord Stainton said not too quietly, his wife nodding in agreement.

"No matter, the Pharoah's Sapphire is safe now," Sam said, and he smiled reassuringly and tapped on his breast pocket.

"Speaking of mind reading and such things, did you know Bertie that Lady Stainton is now able to predict the future?"

"No, I didn't know that, how interesting."

"It's more than interesting, it's amazing. It all started a short while back when we were at a little soirée at your parents' home. There was that singer there, Tom Jones. Anyway, we got talking to this chap and your aunt was telling him how she enjoyed spending time in the garden and how she talked to the plants and the trees, and her regular conversations with Raymond."

"Raymond?" Sam said inquisitively.

"Yes, one of the koi carp in our garden pond, he is nearly ten years old. Anyway, this chap was clearly surprised and just before he was called away on urgent business and had to rush out of the house, he suggested that your aunt should develop her skills. Long story short we engaged this person who apparently is related to Nostradamus. She must be I reckon because between you and me she charges a small fortune for her weekly tutoring. That said your aunt has come on leaps and bounds."

"Amazing," Sam said.

"I know," Lord Stainton replied, and turning to his wife said, "Go on dear, predict the future."

Lady Stainton gave an expression of concentration and said,

"I predict we are all about to have dinner and tomorrow we will all be in Venice."

"There you go. How about that?" Lord Stainton said proudly.

"Unbelievable," Sam said.

"That's just what that man at the soirée said. What do you think James?"

"I imagine being able to predict future events could be a very useful attribute, Lord Stainton."

"Oh, it is, it is."

And so, the evening slowly went by.

Finally, it was time for bed. Unfortunately, however, when Sam stood up to leave, so did Frankie Doyle who gave Sam a strange look.

"Don't I know you?" Frankie said.

"No, you don't know me. But you did lock me in your storeroom once. Tell me, did you manage to get the fire put out?" Sam said and turned around as best he could with a plastered leg and with the aid of his crutch hobbled back to his cabin.

7.

Returning to their cabin Sam and James found that it had indeed been transformed into their sleeping quarters for the night.

"Well, this all looks rather cosy," Sam said.

"It does indeed, sir."

"Now," Sam said, rubbing his hands together and looking about the room, "Where are we going to put this damn stone for safe keeping?"

"Where, indeed, sir."

"You know I once read that the best place to hide something is in plain view. So, I think I will simply place it on this small table next to my bed," Sam said.

"I do believe there is a certain amount of risk inherent in your strategy, sir."

"That is because you don't understand the criminal mind as I do, James."

"Just as you say, sir."

"There we go," Sam said placing the stone under the small lamp on the table next to the cabin window.

"You know what, James?"

"No, sir."

"Right now, I just fancy a nightcap, a brandy would be nice, I think it may help me sleep. Would you mind popping back along to the bar car and getting me one. And one for yourself of course if you would like one."

"Thank you, sir," and James left their quarters and made his way down the carriage corridor. Meanwhile, Sam got washed and changed and, manoeuvring his plastered leg around the top bunk bed ladder, clambered into the lower bunk bed.

After a short while James returned, carrying a small silver tray upon which was balanced a large glass of brandy.

"Thank you, James," Sam said, taking the drink. He sat upright in his small bed with his back resting against his soft pillows which he had arranged behind him. Sam sipped his brandy and listened to the rhythmic sound of the train as it raced through the French countryside.

"Funny things jewels," Sam suddenly said.

"Sir?"

"Well, we dig them out of the ground, pay a small fortune for some of them, some people are prepared to risk losing their freedom by stealing them, and what for? To hang around our neck or such like. We live in a topsy turvy world, James."

"It does seem that way at times, sir."

Sleep naturally followed.

…..……………

Sam slowly opened his eyes and focused on the bunk bed above him. He gathered his thoughts, he was on the Orient Express, on his way to Venice where they would arrive later today, and he was guarding the Pharoah's Sapphire.

"Good morning, sir," a familiar voice said, "I have taken the liberty of bringing you a strong cup of coffee."

"Oh, thank you James, that is very thoughtful."

"I thought it best in the circumstances," James replied.

"Circumstances? What do you mean?"

"The jewel, sir. It is gone."

"What? Where?" Sam said, with a look of horror on his face and hastily looking under his bed and on the floor of the cabin.

"Oh, heck, what are we going to do?" Sam said anxiously.

"With respect sir, I suggest we do nothing."

"Nothing James? But we have been robbed. The Pharoah's Sapphire is gone. What will my aunt and uncle say? I bet it was that Frankie Doyle."

"If I may be so bold as to contradict you sir, the Pharoah's Sapphire has not been stolen. It is only a copy of the stone, a glass jewel which has in fact been stolen. Although the person who now has this in their possession naturally believes it to be the original stone."

"You are confusing me, James."

"As per your instruction, I collected the Pharoah's Sapphire from Lord and Lady Stainton yesterday, but before I gave it to you sir, I substituted it for a copy, an imitation stone."

"But where did you get that?" Sam asked.

"Recognising the real risk of the stone being stolen, I took the opportunity when we recently visited Lord and Lady Stainton to photograph the stone. I then passed the photographs to a friend of a friend who made a perfectly acceptable glass duplicate."

"Good thinking James."

"Thank you, sir."

"But hold on. How did the thief, whoever it was, know we had the stone?"

"When in the Bar Car last evening I also took the opportunity of mentioning that not only were you related to Lord and Lady Stainton, but you had also agreed as the good nephew, to look after their valuables on this trip. I calculated this information would make its way to the miscreant. Subsequent events proved that this was the case."

"But why?"

"I felt sure that rather than Lord and Lady Stainton suffer the potential trauma of possibly encountering a thief, that you would prefer any such a concurrence to be with yourself, sir."

"Fair enough I suppose," Sam said nodding in agreement, "So where is the Pharoah's Sapphire now?"

James took the stone from his inside jacket pocket and handed it over. Sam opened the small velvet box,

"Very nice," he said and closed the box again.

"Nice coffee," Sam confirmed and took another sip.

. . . .

It was not long before the Orient Express came to a gentle halt at Venezia Santa Lucia train station, next to the Grand Canal in Venice. As Sam and James stepped from the train Frankie Doyle and a very slim man with short cropped hair and pointed features walked by, both wore a smug expression and said nothing. Sam did his best to ignore them but couldn't help smiling. He turned his attention instead to Claude who was standing by the carriage door. Sam thanked him for his attentive service and wished him well. Claude in turn thanked James for his tip for removing wax from linen gloves.

Further along the busy station platform Sam caught sight of his aunt and uncle and hurried along to see them.

"There you are," Sam said proudly, "One Pharoah's Sapphire, safe and sound," and handed the jewel over to his aunt.

"Oh, thank you Bertie, it was kind of you to look after it for me." "It was my pleasure. No trouble at all," Sam replied with a grin.

Turning to James, Sam said,

"All's well that ends well, eh James?"

"Indeed, sir."

Stephen Towers

The Casebook of Private Investigator Sam Sloane

The School Charter

Stephen Towers

1.

Despite earlier that day having demonstrated his resolve to losing some weight by refusing a second piece of Terry's chocolate orange, walking past the open door the aroma from within was simply over powering, and without further thought Sam joined the queue standing inside the fish and chip shop.

The chip shop was under new management and the word on the street was it was good, far better than it was under the previous owners who it was rumoured kept a flatulent pig behind the counter as an air freshener. Apparently, things had come to a head when a customer was served a battered finger with their chips and curry sauce. The local press naturally made a meal out of it and the owners sold up and quickly moved on, to Barbados it was said, where Mr Jenkins, the previous owner, now drove a taxi, and his wife sold knock off DVDs and played bingo with her good hand.

Sam had been feeling a little lethargic of late, and having recently found that he had to fasten his trouser belt on the last available hole, he had decided he would try and lose a couple of pounds. Now, waiting in the chip shop queue ready to place his order, he was starting to experience feelings of guilt and self-reproach. After some very brief soul searching, he decided he would as a surprise also take some chips back to the office for his secretary, Barbara, and his negative feelings were soon replaced by a feel-good sensation – with Sam portrayed as the kind and thoughtful boss.

It was a blustery, damp day and the plastic bag containing his lunch swung uncontrollably as he walked. Entering his office, he found not only that some of the logo colours from the plastic bag had made their way onto his beige raincoat, but also that Barbara was sitting at her desk with a brown paper bag over her head covering her face.

"Hello, Barbara, what are you doing and why do you have a bag over your face?" Sam asked.

"Oh, hello Mr Sloane, I wasn't sure you would notice," Barbara replied in a surprised tone.

"Well, as an experienced private investigator I tend to notice such things."

"Well, the thing is, I have bought this expensive night cream which is supposed to stop you getting wrinkles. But I am going out tonight and probably won't be back until late and so won't be able to try it out. So, I thought if I put some on now and put this bag over my head to pretend it was night time, I could see if it worked."

"I have brought you some chips," Sam replied.

"Oh, that is the nice smell," Barbara said, removing the paper bag. "There is some salt and vinegar in the kitchen cupboard. I will go and get it." And she hurried out excitedly. Returning to her office she accidentally spilt some salt.

"Ooops," Barbara said, and she bent down and threw some of the spilt salt over her shoulder.

"What are you doing?" Sam asked.

"It's bad luck to spill salt and if you do you have to throw some over your shoulder or something like that," Barbara replied, very matter of factly.

"Superstitious nonsense," Sam said and laughed.

"No, it isn't. My cousin Raymond spilt some salt. Next thing he knew his foot fell off. He was cleaning some mud off his boots and his foot just dropped off."

"Goodness me, how awful. As a matter of interest what was he cleaning his boots with?"

"A chainsaw. So, you can't be too careful. Do you check your horoscope?"

"No," Sam replied.

"Well, you should. Let us see what yours has to say today," Barbara said, opening her newspaper. "Aries, Aries, Aries, here we are. It says you are to receive some unexpected news in the post."

"I bet it's not an apology letter from the Inland Revenue with a large cheque attached," Sam said, smiling. "Anyway, speaking of getting things in the post, it's my mother's birthday and I forgot to post her card so I am going to have to deliver it in person later today."

"Can't you just post it so she gets it tomorrow. Or will she be upset if she doesn't get it today?" Barbara innocently enquired.

"Barbara, my mother believes the Spanish Inquisition was just tough love for heretics. What do you think?"

"Nice chips," Barbara replied.

………………..

As anyone who has tried it will testify, and as Sam soon discovered, riding your bicycle on a windy day while carrying a bunch of flowers is not a good idea.

When Sam arrived outside the tall gates of his parent's home, his only surprise when he examined his mother's birthday gift was that the flowers had not left a suicide note. He entered the gate security code, the gates slowly opened, and he cycled up the long gravel drive to the front door where he was greeted by the butler, James.

"Good evening, sir, I do hope you are well."

"Yes, thank you James. I thought I would surprise my mother on her birthday. I have brought her these flowers, but unfortunately, they have got rather battered by the wind."

Looking down at the forlorn bunch held by Sam, James agreed,

"So I see sir. May I suggest that you consider exchanging them with these flowers which a courier has only just left. Thereby not diminishing in any way your original thoughtful intention."

"Sounds like a good idea. Who are those flowers from James?"

"They are from the company who supplied the ice sculpture of Lady Edgeware on the occasion of her birthday sir."

"Sounds appropriate. They were probably included in their bill anyway."

"Indeed, sir."

"Okay James, you lose their greeting card and get rid of these." Sam handed James what was left of the bunch of flowers he had brought and took the flower arrangement supplied by the ice sculpture company.

"Very well, sir."

"Well done, James, you are a godsend."

"I endeavour to please, sir. Lord and Lady Edgeware and the Earl and Countess of Dupree are in the drawing room."

Sam's shoulders sank and his eyes rolled up. The ancestors of the Earl and Countess of Dupree had only just managed to escape France and the guillotine at the time of the French revolution. Unfortunately however, despite the passage of time, their descendants still held more than a grudge. They never bought anything manufactured in France and still looked down on the "common people" or "peasants" as they referred to them believing them to be the cause of all problems, including the Earl's gout.

Sam made his way across the spacious entrance hall passing numerous birthday cards which were on display. He calculated that on the basis of the age shown on some of the cards that it was only a matter of time before his mother was younger than him. Outside the drawing room he straightened up, put on his best smile and opened the heavy room door.

"Happy birthday mother, I have brought you these."

"But no card that I can see," Sam's mother replied.

"It's on the table in the hall, the one you bought in Paris," Sam said.

"Paris!" the Earl exclaimed.

"The table was made in Sri Lanka," Sam's mother blurted apologetically.

"You have met my son, haven't you?" Lord Edgeware interjected, trying to change the topic.

"Ah, yes, I believe I have. What have you been up to young fellow?"

"He has been doing a lot of travelling," Sam's father quickly responded.

"See the world, that's the ticket. Not France mind you, horrible place, nasty people, can't trust them, turn your back on them and they want to hack your head off. If you ask me ……"

"Can I get you a refill?" Sam's father interrupted, gesturing toward the Earl's glass of whisky.

"Don't mind if you do. A cheeky little vintage this isn't it. Kind of creeps up on you, rather like a Japanese sniper," the Earl replied, struggling to heave his large body forward in his chair and eventually giving up and sinking back down.

"Did I tell you what happened to us on the way to the airport recently?" the Earl asked but before anyone responded he continued, "Well, we were in the Rolls, making our way along the M25 when we were forced to slow down. There had been an accident of some sort with a couple of those domestic cars, I think they call them hatchbacks. Anyhow, when we got up close, I noticed one of the vehicles was from France. Well, I opened the car window and said to the fireman who was cutting the driver out, the accident would have been his fault he is French, just throw him in the ditch. Well, I could see the fireman appreciated my advice. I don't mind helping my fellow man if I can. In fact, only just recently I gave someone collecting for something called the Salvation Army my old cigar cutters."

Sam turned to his mother and said,

"I understand you had an ice sculpture delivered."

"Yes, but when it started to melt, I had to have one of the servants destroy it, it made me look as if I had bingo wings. That reminds me, those ice sculptors said they would send me some flowers and I haven't seen any. They had better not forget."

"Probably arrive tomorrow," Sam proffered.

After what seemed to Sam to be a polite length of time and not so short as to give the impression that he was eager to leave, he wished everyone present a pleasant evening and absented himself from the gathering. Closing the drawing room door behind him he took a large intake of breath and made his way across the hall to the front door of his parent's home, where he was met by James.

"Excuse me sir, but this postal correspondence arrived for you today."

Sam opened the small envelope to find an invitation to a school reunion.

"Well, I never did," Sam exclaimed, and carefully placed the invitation back in the envelope, which he put in his inside pocket and cycled home, wondering what such a reunion would have in store.

2.

Somehow the metal gates to Sam's old school didn't seem as tall as he recalled, and the lions which sat upright on top of the gate pillars didn't seem as ferocious or foreboding as they did on his first day at Topley Towers Boarding School for Boys.

It had been quite a surprise when his parents had dropped him off all those years ago. They had never mentioned to him that he was going to boarding school. He remembered feeling rather confused and more than a little uneasy when his parents drove off leaving him there. His nanny had always taught him never to talk to strangers and if he found himself with one to always run to the person he knew. Well, with a screech of tyres his parent's car had sped off at a fair speed and he didn't think he would be able to catch it.

"Come with me Master Edgeware," the tall man with what seemed to be an insincere smile had said, and young Bertram Edgeware had little option.

Topley Towers was an impressive looking building but expensive to maintain and heat, as the boys who attended the school knew only too well, often kept awake by the chattering teeth of those they shared their small dormitory with. The extensive grounds within which it stood were equally imposing although potentially dangerous if you happened to fall into one of the many large holes dug by Mr Symmonds, the Geography Master.

Mr Symmonds had a phobia of Black Bears. He had developed this when he had been hiking the Appalachian Trail in America and a bear got caught in one of his tent's guy ropes one night and brought down part of his tent. As a result, in order to ease his mind, he had dug numerous bear traps around the school.

As Sam walked up the tree-lined drive to the school, he pondered who would be attending the reunion. It had been many years since he had seen most of his classmates and he wondered what they would look like now. Sam consciously pulled his stomach in and his trousers up.

Climbing the stone steps as he had done numerous times before as a young pupil, Sam entered his old school through the large arched doorway. Standing in the entrance foyer with its highly polished parquet floor it seemed as if very little if anything had changed. A shiver ran down his spine. Then a soothing, familiar voice said,

"It's Bertram Edgeware isn't it."

"Yes, Miss," Sam instinctively replied, and suddenly realised that he was talking to Mrs Grainger, the school nurse from years back. When Sam had attended Topley Towers, Nurse Grainger was the source of protection from Mr Lawrence the games master, who was believed to be a direct descendant of Vlad the Impaler. It seemed to the boys at the school that Mr Lawrence took great enjoyment from inflicting pain under the questionable guise of "…it will toughen them up." He would arrange rugby practice when the temperature was at least five degrees below freezing and cross country running during severe thunderstorms. Boys who failed to perform well were required to do one hundred press ups over an ant hill while covered in chocolate. Or, weather permitting, climb the local church steeple during a lightning storm. Nurse Grainger would provide the absence notes excusing boys from games.

On this occasion she was handing out the name badges to the reunion attendees. And no doubt as she did so, still receiving many deep-felt expressions of gratitude for the absence notes from former pupils.

"So far I have managed to recognise everyone who has come through that door," she said, proudly.

"You must have an excellent memory," Sam replied, pinning on his name badge. "Where is the reunion?"

"It's in the refectory, but the headmaster has asked if you wouldn't mind seeing him before you go through. He is in his office. Do you remember where that is?"

"Oh yes, on more than one occasion I have sat nervously outside that office door. Tell me who is the headmaster these days?"

"Mr Donald."

"Still? My goodness, he must be an age. Does he still wear his black teaching gown and mortar board all of the time? Sad really, what sort of a life is that? Well, I suppose it takes all sorts," Sam said, laughing.

"Mr Donald and I got married."

"Nice man, a credit to the teaching profession I have always thought. He has been my life role model," Sam quickly said while nodding in insincere admiration. Mrs Donald had however obviously turned her attention to silently arranging the remaining name cards.

A rather embarrassed Sam made his way up the grand staircase, past the glass cabinet of cups and shields annually awarded to outstanding pupils, past the large hanging portraits of previous headmasters, to the all-too familiar (for Sam) four ancient wooden chairs which sat facing each other outside the headmaster's office. Sam moved one of the chairs and there it was, the spot where one day, waiting to be admonished for telling lies, he had with a small penknife inscribed his initials "B.E." in the wooden wall panelling. During a music lesson he had told Porky George that pie eating aliens had landed. And as a result, George had run out of class and locked himself in the toilet and refused to come out until he had consumed all of the contents of a large food hamper recently sent to him by his parents.

Sam knocked on the solid mahogany door.

"Come in," an authoritative voice called out.

Sam turned the brass door knob and the door creaked open to reveal a room which was just as Sam recalled. It too appeared to have been frozen in time. It was musty smelling, very dim and dingy, the small window with its heavy curtains restricting much of the natural light. A dark wood bookcase covered one wall, there were several filing cabinets against another and what appeared to be a small drinks cabinet next to them. In the centre of the room was a large, grand desk and behind this stood Mr Donald, the headmaster, who held a well-practised still pose until Sam had fully entered, and then held out his hand and smiled.

"Bertram, very nice to see you again. How are you keeping?"

"I am well, thank you, headmaster," Sam said, shaking the headmaster's hand.

"Please call me Mr Donald."

"Very well. Nice to see you too after all these years Mr Donald. I met your wife on my way in. Of course, I knew her as Nurse Grainger."

"Ah yes, of course. We bumped into one another at a sex addiction class some years back now and soon realised we had a number of things in common. Please sit down, you are no doubt wondering why I asked to see you. So, l will get straight to the point and explain," Mr Donald said with a very serious expression. "For many years now, this school has benefited from a Charter which amongst other things allows it to remain on this site. The only stringent non-negotiable proviso being that every ten years we are required to present this Charter to the local magistrate and for them to sign a statement to the effect that they have seen it. What I tell you now is in the strictest confidence. The Charter which up until recently hung on my office wall, has gone missing."

Sam looked at the wall and there was indeed a discolouration on the paintwork and a number of cobwebs where a large picture frame had obviously once hung.

"Now, I understand that you are a private investigator," Mr Donald continued. "Do you think you would be able to locate the missing Charter? I dare not tell the Police because if word got out, I shudder to think what the impact could be. We are due to present the Charter in three weeks' time and if we cannot do so we could lose the school. In fact, I understand a local builder is already preparing plans for the redevelopment of this site. Although how he found out about our predicament I do not know. I was planning to retire next year, between you and me my eye sight is getting rather bad, and losing the school would be a terrible way to end my time at Topley Towers. Bertram, can you help us?"

"Rest assured headmaster, er Mr Donald I will do whatever I can to locate it. When exactly did the Charter disappear?"

"Six weeks ago today, the eighth of May. I remember because I had just been for my regular colonic irrigation appointment. I never miss. Have you tried it?"

"Er, no," Sam replied rather skittishly.

"I would recommend it young Bertram; it can put a real spring in your step."

"I imagine it would. I will put it on my Things to Do List," Sam replied, smiling. "I don't suppose you have a photograph of the Charter? Then at least I know what I am looking for."

"Erm, let me think. Yes, I do," the headmaster said while rummaging in one of his desk drawers. "Here it is, you may recognise the person holding the framed Charter, it's Mr Gilmore. He would have taught you year one biology."

"Vaguely, was he the one with the unusually tall wife," Sam replied.

"No, not exactly."

Sam gave what was obviously a confused expression and asked,

"Will he be at the reunion?"

No, and that is the strange thing. On the same day the Charter disappeared so did Mr Gilmore. Never heard nor seen hide nor hair of him since that day. His rooms were just left. He never even left a note."

"Well, if it is okay with you headmaster, that is where I would like to start. Would it be possible to look around Mr Gilmore's rooms?"

"Of course, Bertram. But what about the reunion with your classmates?"

"Oh, I don't imagine I will be very long. Then I can join my old classmates after that," Sam replied, smiling.

3.

Sam and the headmaster climbed the well-trod uncarpeted wooden stairs to the rooms of the residential teaching staff which were on the top floor of the house. Outside room 14 the headmaster stopped.

"These are Mr Gilmore's rooms." Then as he put the door key into the lock he paused. "Before we go in there is something I feel I should tell you."

Sam looked at the headmaster quizzically.

"Mr Gilmore liked horse racing."

"The sport of kings, eh? What is so unusual about that, that you feel the need to tell me?"

"Well, Mr Gilmore particularly liked Ladies Day. You see he regularly dressed up as a woman. Which is one of the reasons people didn't see him around the school much. He was actually around, but as Loretta. In fairness he did make a very good Loretta. In fact, on more than one occasion he was almost picked up when he visited the local village pub."

"Yes, I remember now," Sam said, "I thought that was Mr Gilmore's wife. I recall being really impressed how she could pick up a medicine ball with just one hand. Mr Gilmore must have been at the school a number of years now." Sam remarked.

"Yes indeed, in fact he joined us at Topley Towers soon after he left university. He has always been very supportive of the school. He once won a bet that he could run a half marathon in high heel shoes to raise funds for the school. Not many people know this but after he joined us here, I discovered Mr Gilmore was actually distantly related to the founders of this school."

"Really? Small world."

Opening the door, they found a room which gave a very good impression of having been ransacked.

"My goodness, what do you think has happened in here?" the headmaster asked.

"Well, either Mr Gilmore was a very untidy person comfortable with the post-gas-explosion look, or this room has been thoroughly searched by someone unknown for something as yet unknown, or, Mr Gilmore wants to give the impression that the room has been thoroughly searched for something. At this stage I would have to say, take your pick."

Mr Donald and Sam slowly picked their way around the rooms, carefully stepping over the books, ornaments, and women's underwear which littered the floor.

"May I ask what it is we are looking for?" the headmaster said.

"I don't know yet," Sam replied, lifting a pink feather boa which was covering some eye shadow pallets on top of a table stool. "Something out of the ordinary."

"Well, that could be a number of things in here," the headmaster remarked, while answering his ringing phone.

"Hello…. yes dear…. oh, I see…. I will be right there."

"I do apologise Bertram, but I am needed elsewhere. Do you mind if I leave you to it?"

"No, not at all. I will let myself out."

With that the headmaster turned and hurried away, his black master's gown wafting up as he did so. Sam continued his search. He sat himself down at the small desk by the window and pulled open one of the desk drawers, totally oblivious to the curtain behind him slowly moving. Suddenly Sam felt a sharp pain in his neck and rubbing it he discovered and pulled out what looked like a small homemade blowgun dart. As he examined the dart his vision quickly became blurred.

The next thing Sam knew he was lying in a twisted heap on the floor. As he lay there, he tried to gather his thoughts. He recalled sitting at the desk, opening a drawer and then feeling a sharp pain in his neck. There was a small dart. With some difficulty he moved one of his arms and managed to rub his neck, which he found painful to the touch and obviously swollen. Still lying on the floor and a little hesitant to move in case he discovered more pain, his eyes finally fully focused. He thought he could see what looked like a book taped to the underside of one of the desk drawers. Slowly moving his other arm, he removed it. Clearly whoever had done this was anxious to ensure the book for whatever reason remained secret. Sam slowly pulled himself up and managed to sit back in the desk chair. Still rather groggy he looked about the floor beside him for the dart which had stuck him but he could not see it. He gazed about the room and as he did so he realised that the light was somehow different, he checked his watch, it was almost 8.00am. He had been unconscious for over twelve hours.

Although Sam wasn't what he would describe as a party animal, in fact he generally looked for a reasonable excuse why he couldn't attend parties, he had been looking forward to meeting some of his old school chums, and so was disappointed that he had now missed the reunion. He decided when this missing Charter case was concluded he would make the effort to contact his old friends, as he had resolved to do so on more than one occasion previously, usually when he had a drink or two, when it always seemed a good idea, but this time he told himself he would follow through, and like his diet he was resolved to stick to it.

Sam turned his attention to the book he had found. On an otherwise plain cover was hand written the number 17. Leafing through the pages Sam soon realised that it was a diary. Could this have been what the person who had searched the rooms have been looking for? And did that same person or persons fire that dart into his neck? Sam decided it would be best to leave the rooms without delay. He slipped the book into his side jacket pocket and made his way back to the headmaster's office.

"Good morning, Bertram, did you enjoy the evening?"

"In a word, no," Sam replied and relayed as best as he could recall what had happened. "But I have found this," Sam said pulling the diary from his pocket, "which may provide us with a clue, it appears to be a diary. Is there somewhere where I can sit and study it?"

"Use my office, I have to go out and will be out for a couple of hours at least. And you are sure you don't want someone to look at your neck?"

"No, I am fine now thank you."

"I will see if I can arrange for some coffee and something to eat to be brought up to you. There is bound to be things left from last night. Oh, it is such a shame you missed it."

Sam sat down at the headmaster's desk and began leafing through the diary. After two cups of coffee and some pepperoni pizza balls, prawn vol-au-vents, and sausage rolls, he found he was able to piece together some extracts from the diary. A theme was clearly emerging.

March 10th – Clearly R is unhappy about something today. Banging doors loud enough to wake the dead. Wonder what is wrong with him?

March 21st – That could have been tricky! Almost got picked up by R at the local pub tonight. He was as drunk as a lord. Saw him in deep conversation with that local builder with the dodgy reputation. Can't be anything good come from that. Anyway, Loretta's reputation remains unblemished.

April 4th – Saw R and his wife in a car showroom – both looked very dapper. Must have come into some money! His wife was wearing some lovely shoes. I wonder where she got them?

April 22ⁿᵈ – Discovered R alone in headmaster's office. He seemed rather embarrassed to have been found there. I wonder what he was up to? Told headmaster who didn't know either. Think I will keep an eye on him.

May 7ᵗʰ – Something is going on and I don't know what. Caught that unscrupulous builder snooping around the school grounds today. He claimed he had lost his dog. Later discovered he doesn't have a dog. Bumped into R's wife who for some reason seemed a bit self-conscious to see me. I didn't ask her about the shoes. Something is afoot and it isn't twelve inches. Sorry I couldn't resist that.

May 8ᵗʰ – Went to see headmaster earlier this morning re new timetable but forgot it was his colonic irrigation day. I noticed school Charter missing from his office wall and later saw R carrying a large package. Probably totally innocent but I think I will use my free period this afternoon to investigate further.

It was almost noon when the headmaster returned to his office.

"Hello Bertram, how are you getting on? Any luck?"

"Who is R?"

4.

"Oh yes, I am sure everyone knew about Mr Gilmore's diaries," the headmaster said. "We used to regularly rib him about them. Those and his fascination with ancestry. I think everyone secretly hoped that he would discover they were related to royalty. He didn't write anything negative about me in his diaries, did he?"

"No, I have not found anything like that," Sam replied assuringly.

"And no mention or hint as to why he just disappeared?"

"Again, nothing I am afraid. Which suggests his disappearance was not planned. We will clearly need to dig a little deeper on that."

"About the Charter, I hear what you say about it probably being an inside job, but I really struggle to understand why anyone here would do it, what is their possible motive?" the headmaster asked.

"At this stage I would guess money. The site on which this school stands is a very attractive one, and I would imagine it is worth a small fortune. More so when developed with lots of small, but no doubt marketed as *exclusive executive homes*."

"No, we must prevent that at all costs. We can't have people digging up this site, you never know what they might find. You know what people are like, they will jump to conclusions. I didn't know he was a war criminal. I needed the money and…." The headmaster stopped himself, and then continued, "sorry about that, just slipped out. Where were we?"

With a rather puzzled look, Sam said,

"You were going to tell me who R might be."

"Oh yes, the headmaster said, rubbing his chin thoughtfully. "Well, we have Roger Watkins, the physics master, Thomas Rainworth, economics, and Reverend Crompton, religious education. They are the only people employed by the school with an R in the initials of their name or in the case of the vicar in his job title."

"Well, it's a start. By the way, to your knowledge have any of them recently purchased a new car?"

"No, not that I am aware of," the headmaster replied while carefully cleaning the lenses of his spectacles. Why do you ask?"

"Mr Gilmore has written that he saw R in a car showroom with his wife. No matter, it may be nothing, I just thought it might have given us the break that we need. What about this local builder referred to in the diary?"

"Mr Briggs. I have never met him. But from what I hear he seems to be a person who generally gets what he wants. And has a reputation for sometimes employing dubious means in order to do so. But I hasten to add that nothing has ever been proven so don't quote me on that. I don't fancy the idea of waking up with a horse's head in my bed. I mean how would you ever get the stains out?"

"Well, according to Mr Gilmore's diary, R met with Mr Briggs and so he may be able to tell me who R is. So, I think I will pay him a visit. Do you know where I can find him?"

"Yes, his offices are in the centre of the village. It is a very grand building with a pillared entrance. Lots of gargoyles."

"Sounds rather out of keeping with the rest of the village. I am surprised he got planning approval for that."

"So is everyone else. The planning officer who gave permission for it disappeared soon after, and has never been seen or heard from since."

....

Sam made his way out of the school and headed toward the nearby village of Topley. On the way he took out his mobile phone and rang his secretary, Barbara.

"Hello Barbara it's Sam."

"Oh, hello Mr Sloane, did you enjoy your reunion party? Did you meet all of your old school friends? And get hammered? Did you get so drunk you woke up in a mortuary with a chimpanzee?"

"Actually, no."

"It happened to me once, I think I was in Morocco. Or was it, Chipping Norton? Anyway, the chimpanzee was called Yoko, or was it Dando? Funny how you remember some things and not others. I remember once..."

"Yes, isn't it," Sam interrupted. "Now I need you to check if a Jonathan Gilmore whose address will be Topley Towers school, has used his passport or any of his credit cards since 8th May. Ring me back and let me know as soon as you find out. Must dash, bye." Sam wasn't in the mood for a lengthy conversation and this one had already proved too long.

Sam soon found himself standing outside the ostentatious entrance of Briggs Developments. He pressed the doorbell which rang very loud to the tune of "Agadoo". Moments later the front door was opened by a young woman who looked very much like a life size Barbie doll.

"Hello, how may I help you?" she asked in a very high-pitched voice, so loud that a number of neighbourhood dogs came running.

"I would like to see Mr Briggs please," Sam said.

"Come in. Whom should I say is calling?"

"Sam Sloane, it's about a personal matter."

"Please follow me."

Sam stepped inside, closed the door behind him and followed the Barbie lookalike across the entrance foyer. She stopped outside one of the room doors then gently knocked and said,

"Mr Briggs, there is a Sam Sloane here to see you with a personal problem."

"Send him in please, Trudi," a voice from within the room said.

Sam entered to find an impeccably dressed middle aged man sitting in an armchair, drinking a glass of milk.

"Please sit down Mr Sloane," the man said, pointing Sam in the direction of another armchair. "People often find it strange that I enjoy a glass of milk but it is good for my indigestion. Unfortunately, in life we sometimes have to do unpleasant things. I hate to tell you some of the unpleasant things I have had to do. This upsets me and this affects my digestion. My fiancée, Trudi, who you met on your way in, tells me milk is good for soothing an acidic stomach, so I have a regular glass."

"She clearly looks after you," Sam said as he sat down.

"We met at a boxing match which I was promoting following the sudden death of a business associate."

"Sudden death?" Sam said.

"Well, he wasn't expecting it. Anyway, enough of me, how may I help you?"

"Well, erm, it's like this. A friend of mine has gone missing and I hoped you might be able to help me find him."

"Me Mr Sloane? What makes you think I can help, surely this is a job for the Police?"

"Unfortunately, so far, the Police have been unable to locate him."

"What's his name?"

"Gilmore, Jonathan Gilmore. He works at Topley Towers school."

"I am afraid I know of no one of that name."

"He drinks in the local village pub which I understand you sometimes frequent. I thought while in there you may have chatted to people from the school?"

"I am sorry Mr Sloane; I do not know anyone from the school. Is there anything else I can help you with? Would you like a glass of milk?"

"No thank you, I have probably taken up enough of your time already," Sam said, standing up from the chair.

"I will show you out. Would you like to see my builder's yard? It is at the rear of these premises. I think you will find it impressive."

Without waiting for a response Mr Briggs guided Sam down a long corridor and through a large timber door, but as Sam stepped through it a large steel wrecking ball flew past him almost knocking him off his feet.

"Careful Mr Sloane, you could have been badly injured or even killed. You must be more careful; builders' yards can be dangerous places."

"That was a close one, wasn't it?" Sam replied, a little shaken. "I think I owe you one for pulling me back as you did."

"Not at all Mr Sloane I was glad to help. Maybe one day you will be in a position to help me?"

"Yes, of course, anything. Just ask."

"Tell me then, has the headmaster found his Charter yet?"

5.

Making his way back to his old school Sam concluded three things:

Firstly, Mr Briggs clearly knew a lot more than he said, but had no intention of sharing any relevant information;

Secondly, Mr Briggs was not the sort of person you would want to cross unless you had become very tired of life;

Thirdly, be wary of and always give way to wrecking balls.

Sam's phone rang, it was Barbara.

"Mr Sloane, I have checked into Mr Gilmore as you asked, and he has not used his passport or credit cards since 8th May."

"Thank you, Barbara, that is most useful."

"Also, remember that chimpanzee I was telling you about? Well, his name was Dando. I forgot that I got his name tattooed on my ankle. I can't remember why."

"Okay, thanks Barbara, that is also very useful to know. Now I must dash, bye."

"Bye Mr Sloane."

Sam returned to the headmaster's office, where the head was pacing the floor anxiously waiting for him.

"Any luck?" he asked eagerly as Sam entered the room.

"Unfortunately, not. Mr Briggs clearly knows a lot more than he is saying. But he is playing his cards very close to his chest. I can confirm however that he does know about the Charter."

"You didn't mention my name to him, did you?" the headmaster asked nervously.

"No."

"Thank goodness for that. So, what now?"

"Now, I think I had better meet those three members of staff you mentioned earlier."

"I will let them know you are coming. Should I say why?"

"Tell them it is standard procedure, simply to eliminate them from our enquiries. That usually does the trick."

....

Making his way down one of the school's many corridors Sam could hardly believe his eyes

"My goodness it's Stanley Morgan, isn't it?" Sam said.

"It is sir, can I help you? My word it's Mr Bertram. How are you sir?"

"I am very well thank you. Fancy bumping into you like this. And I take it from the toolbox you are carrying that you are still employed as the school caretaker and still working hard at preventing this school from falling apart?"

"I am indeed sir," he replied laughing. "Started my working life here as an apprentice and never moved on. Never wanted to."

"Tell me, do you still live in the gatehouse?"

"I do indeed sir. You must come and visit me and Mrs Morgan. Did you come for the reunion yesterday?"

"I did indeed."

"Some of you young gentlemen must have had a good time. I am on my way to the refectory now to repair some of the trestle tables. Where are you off to may I ask?"

"I am on my way to visit Roger Watkins."

"Oh, the physics teacher. Well, hopefully I will see you later. Bye for now."

As a pupil of the school Sam had never visited the top floor of Topley Towers where the school masters lived. He never had cause to apart from one occasion when soon after starting at the school he was asked to deliver a note to Mr Symmonds. When Mr Symmonds had opened his room door young Bertram thought he caught a glimpse of Nurse Grainger in an unusual outfit and waving a riding crop. He assumed Mr Symmonds must have been unwell. He did appear to be sweating a lot when he opened his door. Now, returning to the top floor for the second time in as many days Sam knocked on the door of Roger Watkins.

A short, balding, rotund man with a pair of wire glasses balanced on top of his head answered the door. Before Sam could introduce himself, the man said in an impatient voice,

"Come in, come in. Himself rang to say to expect you. Now what is this all about?"

"I am trying to establish people's whereabouts on the 8th May. Would you be able to tell me where you were on that day?"

"How the hell should I know?! Mr Watkin's replied in a disbelieving tone and then continued, "If it was a week day I would be teaching, if it wasn't I have got no idea. Are you able to give me a clue?"

"It was a Tuesday."

"Teaching, there you are, easy, wasn't it? You know that idiot of a headmaster is due to retire next year. Did he tell you that?"

"He did mention it, yes."

"Should have gone years ago. Do you know he promised to recommend me to the governor's board to succeed him. Then three months ago he changed his mind. Swine, I felt sure that job should be mine. I was going to get a new car with the salary hike that would have come with it."

"Oh, have you been looking at cars?" Sam asked.

"All the time. I love cars, don't you?"

"I prefer a bicycle," Sam replied.

"Bloody nuisance if you ask me. Is there anything else you want? I am very busy."

"No that's all for now thank you," Sam replied.

"For now? You mean you might be back?"

"Possibly," Sam said and left.

What a charming man, I should submit his details for consideration as a practice target for contract killers, Sam thought, and continued along the dimly lit corridor to the residence of Thomas Rainworth.

Knocking on the door a nervous voice asked,

"Who is it?"

"It's Bertram Edgeware, I believe the headmaster will have rung to say I was on my way."

The room door was quickly opened, Sam was pulled into the room and the room door was swiftly shut and bolted with several very large bolts. A man wearing a dressing gown then turned to Sam and held out his hand to shake Sam's saying,

"Hello, I am Thomas Rainworth, pleased to meet you."

"Hello," Sam replied, "I presume the headmaster has explained why I am here?"

"Yes, he did," Thomas replied, now staring outside from behind a curtain. "How can I help?"

"Could you tell me where you were on 8th May? It was a Tuesday."

"I would be at school, teaching. I say you don't happen to have a pound coin for my electricity meter, do you?"

"Yes, I think I have," Sam replied, handing over a coin.

"Thanks, I am just experiencing a bit of a cashflow problem at the moment."

"Times can be hard," Sam replied empathising with the teacher.

"You're telling me. I asked the headmaster if there was any chance of an advance on my salary but he refused. I thought his response rather harsh. Particularly when through a contact of mine I was able to secure him a good rate on his regular colonic irrigation appointments. As a result, I had to go to a money lender who now wants the money back and sadly because of a poor investment I don't have it."

"Poor investment?" Sam asked.

"2.30 at Kempton Park yesterday. Lucky Jim they had the nerve to call the horse. I don't think it has finished the race yet."

"Won't they be prepared to give you more time to pay it back?" Sam asked.

"I borrowed the money from the Septic brothers, Bill and Clive, so no chance. They are genetic throwbacks who should live in a pond. In my opinion they have the intellectual capacity of a tuna sandwich."

"Why did you go to them to borrow money?"

"They are my cousins."

"Tricky one," Sam said. "Well, I won't keep you any longer. I can see you are rather pre occupied. If you wouldn't mind letting me out."

....

A crucifix knocker had been fixed to the door of Reverend Crompton's rooms but for some unknown reason Sam felt disinclined to use it to announce his arrival, and knocked gently on the wooden door. Moments later the door opened by a tall white-haired man who gave Sam a warm smile.

"Come in, my son," the reverend said and Sam entered. The walls of the room were covered in African memorabilia, from spears to face masks.

"My word," Sam said looking around, "quite a collection you have here."

"I spent many years in Africa as a missionary. It is where I met my wife. These are my memories. All very fond ones. Have you ever been to Africa?"

"No, I haven't," Sam said, looking carefully around the room for a blowgun.

"It is a wonderful place, but it can also be a cruel place. I miss it enormously. Now I understand through the school grapevine that you would like to know where I was on 8th May?"

"That's right, if you don't mind," Sam replied.

"Well, during term time I have classes on a Tuesday morning, but my afternoons are free. I often give the school caretaker a hand, particularly if he has joinery work in need of doing. Through necessity I started working with wood when I was in Africa and it has become quite a hobby of mine. Strange thing though, I seem to recall on that particular Tuesday Ryton was not about and I couldn't find him anywhere. Maybe he was on holiday? I never thought to ask him afterwards."

"Ryton? I always understood Mr Morgan was called Stanley."

"Ryton is Mr Morgan's first name. For some reason he never uses it, and goes by his middle name Stanley. I think it might have been Mr Gilmore who told me. He found out when he was researching Mr Morgan's family tree."

"I didn't know that," Sam said.

"Oh, yes. Ryton had quite a sorry start to life. He was in Ecuador as a child. His father was an engineer of sorts and he had taken his family out there. There was a tragic accident and both his parents were killed. Ryton was brought up by one of the local indigenous tribes."

"My word," Sam said.

"Thankfully, when he was old enough and with God's guidance, he was able to find his way to Topley Towers and has been here ever since."

"Fortunate indeed," Sam said thoughtfully. "Anyway, thank you very much for your time, I won't bother you any further."

"No bother at all," Reverend Crompton replied.

6.

Upon leaving Reverend Crompton's rooms, Sam decided to make his way down to the school's refectory where Stanley Morgan, occasionally known as Ryton, had mentioned he was going in order to repair some furniture. On his way he passed two neanderthal looking men carrying baseball bats who he assumed to be relatives of Thomas Rainworth. "Keep banging the rocks together guys," Sam thought, and wondered if Thomas had seen them approaching and made good his escape.

Unfortunately, when Sam got to the refectory there was no sign of Stanley and so he resolved to visit the gatehouse, where Stanley and his wife lived. Walking down the path an old Ford Fiesta sped past him leaving a cloud of dust as it did so, it was Thomas Rainworth. Clearly, he must have seen his relatives coming.

The gatehouse wasn't a large dwelling, larger than a modern exclusive executive home, but without the orangery or fitted kitchen. A large purple wisteria grew up its stone walls and around its leaded glass windows, and brightly coloured flowers lined the short path leading to the front door. It had the appearance of a warm, welcoming place.

Sam knocked at the door and wiped his shoes in anticipation of being invited in.

The door opened and Stanley said,

"Mr Bertram, I thought it was you walking up my garden path. Please come in."

Sam entered a small entrance hall from which he was ushered into the living room where a roaring fire burned.

"This is my wife, Mary."

"I am very pleased to meet you Mrs Morgan," Sam said.

"Well, it is very nice to meet you also. Stanley said he had bumped into you. I gather you attended this school as a boy."

"That's right. All those years ago. In some respects, it seems like only yesterday.

Speaking of which, yesterday I met Mrs Grainger she was the school nurse when I attended Topley Towers, I thought she looked well. It made me wonder what happened to some of the masters who taught me, like Mr Symmonds who dug all those bear traps in the school grounds. Do you remember him?"

"Oh yes," Stanley replied. "That was a sad story."

"Sad? In what way?" Sam asked.

"Well, he was killed by a bear while on holiday."

"Oh, did he return to America?" Sam asked.

"No, he was in Grimsby. The bear had escaped from a travelling circus."

"Oh, my word, that is sad, especially having dug all those traps. Tell me, whatever happened to Mr Lawrence? He gave us physical education. He had a cruel streak, I thought."

"That was an interesting story," Stanley said. "He sent one of the boys to climb the local church steeple and the boy got stuck. So, at the insistence of the headmaster, Mr Lawrence had to go up and bring the lad down. Only, when Mr Lawrence got back down all of his hair had turned white. He said when he was up the steeple, he had a vision. Anyway, off he went to become a Trappist monk. We still receive the occasional Christmas card from him."

"Well, I never did," Sam said. "What a place Topley Towers is. You must have seen so much here Stanley, how long have you worked here?"

"All my working life, nearly 50 years. Mary and I have been married over 40 years now. I love this place; I wouldn't want to be anywhere else. What about you Mr Bertram, what have you done since leaving the school?

"I am a private investigator. In fact, although I came here for the school reunion, the headmaster has asked me to look into something. It seems the school Charter has gone missing."

Mrs Morgan started to cry. Through the tears she said,

"Tell him Stanley, tell Bertram. You know it's not right."

"What is it?" Sam asked.

Stanley sighed heavily, he squeezed Mary's hand, and raised his head to meet Sam's gaze.

"I took the Charter, Mr Bertram. I did it in a moment of madness. Mr Donald, the headmaster and I were having a talk and he suggested I should give some thought to retirement. Well, it just came out of the blue. I had never even considered it. Both Mary and I love it here and we don't want to move. Foolishly I know, but I told a builder in the village who said if I gave him the Charter, he promised that we could stay here. So, I took it."

"Have you given the Charter to the builder?" Sam asked.

"No, not yet, I can't bring myself to do it. If I do I know the school may close but if I don't Mary and I will have to move and we don't want to."

"Did the headmaster say you would have to move?"

"Well, no. I just assumed that would be the case. You see I got the house with my job."

"Do you mind if I ask, is Mr Gilmore involved in any way in this?"

Mary burst into tears and Stanley said ashamedly,

"He's downstairs."

"What?" Sam blurted.

Stanley led Sam down into the house cellar, which is something else you don't get with an exclusive executive home. There asleep on a comfortable looking bed was Mr Gilmore.

"Is he drugged?" Sam asked.

"Yes, you see he saw me take the Charter and so I had to keep him quiet until I decided what to do with it."

"Was it you who stuck me with that dart in Mr Gilmore's rooms?"

"Yes, it was. Sorry about that, I panicked. You see I knew Mr Gilmore kept a diary and I wanted to find it in case he had written about seeing me taking the Charter in it. Sorry."

"So, the blowgun and the darts, where did they come from?"

"I learned about those when I was growing up in Ecuador. I made them."

"I see," Sam said, rubbing his neck.

"What should I do Mr Bertram, I know I have done wrong but Mary and I don't want to lose our home."

"Well," Sam said. "If it were me, I would return the Charter to Mr Donald, I am sure he will be delighted to see it. And while you are there ask for clarification on your last conversation. With regard to Mr Gilmore that might be a bit trickier. I would suggest you have a chat with him when he comes to and tell him what you have told me."

7.

It was approaching lunchtime two weeks later and Sam was waiting in the queue of his now favourite chip shop. Standing in front of him and holding a young boy was a man who could easily pass as Frankenstein's twin brother. The boy, while using his nose as a sweet dispensing appliance, stared at Sam who did his best not to catch his gaze. Then quite unexpectedly, a voice from behind him in the queue said,

"Mr Bertram, I thought it was you."

Sam turned.

"Hello Stanley, how are you?"

"I am very well thank you. By the way, I took your advice and saw Mr Donald. He said Mary and I can stop in our home as long as we like. He also wants me to take on an apprentice so when I do decide to retire the apprentice can take over my duties."

"That's excellent news. How may I ask did you get on with Mr Gilmore?" Sam said, pulling a face which suggested he expected a less positive response.

"Well, again as you suggested, I explained why I had done what I did. He wasn't too happy to start with, but then the strangest thing. Mary brought him a cup of tea and he suddenly changed. He said if she would tell him where she bought her shoes, and if she would be prepared to act as his personal shopper, he would forget the whole thing. Well, Mary was more than happy to do so, she loves shopping and between you and me, I am not really that keen on it."

The Casebook of Private Investigator Sam Sloane

A Gambling Problem

1.

Isn't it strange, Sam thought to himself, just as certain smells can seemingly conjure up vivid memories, certain occasions such as attending a funeral, or a Christmas family gathering, can also sometimes make you reflect. Sam was having such a moment. He was sitting in a dentist's waiting room and, despite his best efforts, he could not help but associate his immediate environment and forthcoming experience with pain and discomfort.

Several days earlier an otherwise mild-mannered butterscotch toffee had without malice removed one of Sam's fillings. Although he knew instantly what had happened, he tried to convince himself that it hadn't, or if it had, that it would sort itself out and everything would be fine. Sadly, this fond illusion very soon proved to be just that. As a result, and conscious of the potential likelihood of overdosing on painkillers, he reluctantly accepted that a trip to the dentist was required.

When Sam had contacted his local dental practice, Harmer and Harmer, he had been advised that they could offer him an appointment two weeks on Friday, or if this was unsuitable or he needed an earlier appointment, he could always see Mr Newman, a newly qualified dentist who had recently joined the practice.

Harmer and Harmer was a family dental practice operated by two brothers. It was located just off the town's High Street, and although rumours persisted regarding what went on in their basement at home, nothing had ever been proven and the dental practice remained popular.

Sam had never been to Harmer and Harmer before and when he arrived at the entrance door was rather surprised to find that it appeared to be made of reinforced metal and had a door viewer fitted. Sam hesitantly entered to find a smartly dressed receptionist behind a tall wooden counter.

"Good afternoon," Sam said. "My name is Sam Sloane, I have an appointment to see Mr Newman at 4.30pm."

"Of course, you have," the receptionist replied. and smiled. "Now what sort of drugs would you like?"

"I am sorry," Sam replied a little confused.

"Oh, you are not a regular customer?" the receptionist asked, a little taken aback.

"No, it is my first time here," Sam replied.

"I was wondering if you would like one of our complimentary mugs?" the receptionist quickly said, and coughed, then smiled.

"Oh, no thank you. For a moment there I thought you were trying to sell me some drugs," Sam said, laughing.

"No, certainly not, we definitely don't sell drugs here Mr Sloane, and anyone who says we do is lying and should have their tongues ripped out and nailed to their foreheads. This is a respectable dental practice with no connections whatsoever to any Columbian drug cartels or local gangland leaders. Now please go straight up the stairs, the waiting room is on your right."

Sam slowly climbed the creaking stairs, nervously glancing back at the smiling receptionist as he did so.

To an unenthusiastic squeamish customer, the waiting room was claustrophobically small. Along one wall were six uncomfortable looking wooden chairs, of the sort sold exclusively to dentists and lion tamers. On the wall opposite were several posters on oral hygiene, brushing techniques and the advantages of a totally unnatural looking white smile. And on another wall was a small window which appeared to have been nailed closed. No doubt, Sam thought, to prevent customers escaping before their treatment.

Sam paced around the room, looked out of the small window, and sat down. He checked his watch, it was 4.25pm.

It had been an eventful and certainly unpredictable day so far, Sam thought to himself. While sitting down to breakfast the post had arrived and amongst it was an unexpected and most welcome tax rebate. Then there had been that phone call from his friend, probably his best friend although he had not seen him in a long while, Porky George. And then, upon Sam's arrival at his office, his secretary Barbara had announced that she had found another job. On hearing this news Sam almost fell to his knees to thank God, but somehow managed to restrain his absolute delight, and as soberly as he could, gave the short speech which he had regularly practised over the years. He said how sorry he was she was leaving, and how it would be difficult to find another secretary like her, but wished her all the best for the future and hoped she would remember to visit him if she was ever in the neighbourhood. Sam then slowly went through into his office, closed the door behind him and began running around the room punching the air like a cheerleader on steroids.

....

Sam (who was then still Bertram Edgeware) had first met George Davidson at Topley Towers Boarding School for Boys.

George was a naturally fainthearted but likeable sort of person who was to win brief popularity among the other school boys when he beat Duncan Hogshaw by holding twenty-three gobstoppers in his mouth at one time. And this was despite an overly confident Duncan having surreptitiously had all of his teeth removed the previous night in order to create a larger cavity space – something which had the international judging panel known may well have resulted in Duncan's disqualification, or at the very least a points deduction.

George's parents Edith and Joshua Davidson, owned a sizeable pie factory and a number of butchers' shops, which was fortunate because George had a healthy appetite. Like his parents George suffered from being "big boned" which together with his increasingly tight-fitting clothes prevented him from achieving his full sporting potential at Topley Towers. But, it did earn him his school nickname "Porky George". Needless to say, despite George's parents' protestations, the school headmaster vehemently denied that the school's laundry service was responsible for the shrinkage of their son's uniform.

Bertie and George shared the same dormitory. It was there late one particular night where the increasing sound of George's gurgling stomach was keeping them both awake. They both decided to go down to the school kitchen and see what was available to eat from the fridge. The cook had served steak and kidney pie that day and they were convinced that some would be left and that it had their names on it. So, without switching on any lights, they left the dormitory, and tiptoed along the corridor, down the grand stairs, across the great hall and into the kitchen. As silently as they could they made their way to the large fridge, and were just about to open the door of the kitchen appliance when they heard a noise. The two of them hid behind a bench, and from there saw the school headmaster dressed in only his headmaster's school gown and a pair of Y-fronts enter the kitchen, open the fridge door and remove what was left of the steak and kidney pie. Clearly, he had had the same idea. It was a story they dared not tell but would remember all of their lives.

At that moment sitting in the dentist's waiting room the recollection of that night was a welcome distraction for Sam, and made him smile to himself.

....

Sam wondered what had prompted George to ring him earlier that day. He hadn't wanted to say anything over the telephone other than it was urgent and he needed Sam's help. Sam had explained that he had this dental appointment which he would rather not cancel if he could avoid it. As a result, George agreed to meet Sam in a local pub when he was finished.

The door to the waiting room was pushed fully open.

"Hello, I am Stephen Newman. I guess you must be Mr Sloane my 4.30 appointment."

Sam sat open mouthed at the sight of what looked like a school boy dressed in a light blue tunic. Suddenly he felt quite old. Then having recovered his composure he replied,

"Yes, that's right, I seem to have lost one of my fillings."

"Please follow me and we will take a look," said the dentist and Sam reluctantly did so.

Sam followed the very young-looking dentist into an even smaller room.

"Please sit down," the dentist said pointing (rather unnecessarily, Sam thought) to the large, plastic covered chair with a bright light directly above it. Sam noticed a large poster which had been fixed to the ceiling immediately above him, no doubt as a distraction to patients. It read,

This will not hurt nearly as much as:

1. Being hit by a train,

2. Falling out of a fifth story window,

3. Sawing your leg off,

4. Being torn apart by disgruntled crocodiles, or

5. Having a large wooden stake shoved up your bottom.

So, relax and appreciate how lucky you are.

Sam felt better, momentarily.

"Now open wide," Mr Newman said and peered into Sam's mouth.

"Ah yes, I see. Now I will just give you a little injection to numb the tooth. Then we will see about a new filling."

The dentist disappeared from Sam's line of sight. Sam concentrated on the poster above him reading it over and over again. When Mr Newman reappeared holding a syringe he was visibly shaking.

A now very concerned Sam blurted out,

"If you don't mind me asking, have you done this before?"

"Yes of course, many a time. Well not on a real person, you understand. First time for everything, eh?"

Before Sam could scream, Mr Newman plunged the needle into Sam's gum. While Sam swallowed nervously, the dentist reached for and started his unmistakeable sounding dental drill and, shaking like a leaf in a force nine gale, inserted it into Sam's mouth. Sam felt his eyes fill with tears, how he envied the person being torn apart by crocodiles or falling from a high window.

Moments later Mr Newman announced,

"There you are, all done, that wasn't too bad, was it?"

"No," Sam for some reason unknown to him replied, and wiped the tears from his face.

"Well, if you experience any problems let me know. Otherwise, I will see you in six months for your regular check-up," the dentist said, while wearing a very satisfied look on his face.

2.

The Ship Inn was reputed to be over 500 years old. It was also said that King Charles I had stayed there in 1650, which is questionable as he was beheaded in 1649. Nevertheless, it was a pleasant place, the staff were welcoming, there were no large screen televisions, and you didn't stick to the carpet when you walked across it.

Entering the pub, the pre-arranged rendezvous of the two friends, Sam immediately recognised Porky George. Unsurprisingly he was sitting with a large empty plate on the table in front of him which he was staring at as if in a hypnotic trance.

"George!" Sam exclaimed. His friend's mesmerized concentration was broken and the two of them greeted each other as if they were long lost friends, which of course was exactly what they were. Then, after much laughter and reminiscing, which included the headmaster's-Y-fronts experience, Sam asked,

"So, what is this urgent matter you needed to see me about?"

Suddenly, the blood appeared to drain from George's face and he adopted a very serious, worried expression. He looked about the pub as if to check that no one was listening and quietly said,

"Well, it's like this, Bertie, I have got myself into a bit of a predicament and I need to do an errand."

"An ewand?"

"No, an errand."

"Sowwy," Sam replied. "It's this dental numbing injection, it hasn't yet worn off."

"Can you remember when we were at school and I was forever betting on things? What was going to be served for lunch? How late a master would be for class? That sort of thing. Well, unfortunately when we left school it got out of hand. Long story short, I owe a lot of money and the people I owe it to want it back."

"So, pay them, you're loaded, aren't you?"

"That's just it. I am broke, and I dare not ask my parents again, they bailed me out a few years ago and understandably weren't happy about it then. Don't get me wrong, I don't gamble anymore I have learnt my lesson. The money I owe is an old debt and unfortunately these people don't forget."

"Well, I am afwaid you have caught me a bit short George. I am having a bit of a cash flow problem myself at the minute."

"No, you don't understand. I don't want your money. I just hoped you would accompany me on this errand. You see these people have said if I collect and deliver a certain parcel, they will write the debt off. They assured me that the parcel is nothing illegal, not drugs or weapons or anything like that."

"Well, as you know I am always happy to help a fwiend. When and where is this pick up?"

"Eleven o clock tonight at a disused airfield about forty miles from here."

"Well, that doesn't sound at all suspicious, does it?" Sam said in a sarcastic voice while (to make sure his point was not lost) also raising his eyebrows.

"I know. I will understand totally if you would rather not," George said, fixing Sam with the sort of stare he would more readily associated with an overweight puppy.

"No, count me in," Sam said trying his best to appear enthusiastic, and rubbing his face where he realised there was still a distinct lack of feeling following his recent dental ordeal.

"Are you hungry?" George asked.

"No, I am fine, thanks. Although I wouldn't mind a cup of coffee."

"Well, I will go and get us a coffee and I think I might treat myself to a hot chocolate fudge cake and ice cream which I see they have on their menu."

George got up from their table and went to the bar. Sam sat wondering what he might have got himself in to. What could this package be? Nevertheless, he thought, George was a good friend and needed his help. Sam looked about the pub. A middle-aged couple sat at a table opposite and another similar-aged couple sat down at the table next to them.

"Nice place this," one of the men said to the other couple.

"It is isn't it," the lady replied smiling.

"We have come to meet our son. He is a doctor you know."

"That's nice, our son is a consultant at the local private hospital."

"That's nice. It's all go, isn't it? We have just got back from holiday. Been to Barbados for a month. Lovely weather."

"It usually is, particularly at this time of year. We have a small villa out there."

"Oh, we stayed in a very large villa. We like our space don't we Marjorie. I have some photos of it here," the man said producing his phone.

"Oh, I see you have the old model of that phone. We have the latest model. Here feel the weight," the lady on the next table said, "It is a full twelve grams lighter than the older model. You can really tell the difference. I don't know about you but I can't bear heavy things cluttering up my bag."

"Well, I prefer not to carry a bag these days. I think it is so unfashionable, don't you?" Marjorie replied.

"Well, as a secret agent with a licence to kill, I find it difficult to fit my Walther PPK pistol into my pocket."

"Well, we are related to royalty, so there!"

....

"They are going to bring the coffee over," George said.

"Oh, er great. Sorry I was miles away," Sam replied.

....

Twenty minutes later Sam and George were in George's car travelling toward a disused airfield.

"Any idea how to wemove coffee stains?" Sam asked.

"Afraid not old boy," George replied.

"I had no idea I still had so little sensation in my mouth following my filling."

"Is it a new shirt?"

"I suppose not, but I did like it. Anyway, tell me about these people you owe money to."

"The Bishops," George said with more than a hint of foreboding. "Hard to believe I know, but they are clever, clever and cold blooded. They suck you in. I started going to church in the hope that I would find some distraction from my gambling habit. A bit more meaning to life as it were. Don't get me wrong, they were welcoming enough to start off with. First of all, they have you stacking the hymn books, then it's helping with the church cleaning, then some charity work, you know visiting the sick and needy, that sort of thing. And then before you know it, they have got you."

"Got you?" Sam said quizzically.

"They introduce you to people who manage their gambling dens. That's when you find yourself watching the shadows, scared to go out even. It's not been a pleasant experience, I don't mind telling you, Bertie."

"What about this person we are collecting the package fwom?" Sam asked.

"All I know is that he is called Reggie and he will be at this disused airfield at 11 o clock tonight."

The two friends drove on for a further forty minutes whereupon the car's satnav announced that they had arrived at their destination. It did indeed look like a disused airfield, with areas of lanky grass and weeds growing through joints in the old runway. It was enclosed by a tall wire fence held up by concrete posts. The large metal entrance gates were unlocked and Sam got out of the car and pushed them open. There was a definite chill in the air and a thick mist was forming. Sam returned to the car.

"Better go in?" Sam said.

"Must we?" George replied hesitantly.

"Let's dwive over to those small abandoned buildings. Your contact may well be waiting there," Sam suggested.

"Maybe we should just go home? I will find the money somewhere and pay off my debt. I shouldn't have asked you to come," George said in a mild panic (what he later described as lively revelation).

"Well, it is up to you, but…" Before Sam could finish his sentence, something moved in the shadows. "What's that?" he said pointing.

"I didn't see anything," George said.

"You won't with your eyes closed. Come on, let's check it out."

Sam and George got out of the car and slowly walked toward where Sam thought he had seen some movement. They saw a man dressed in a long overcoat lying on the ground and rushed over to him.

"What happened? Are you okay?" Sam asked.

"I was hit from behind," the man groaned.

"Did you wecognise who did it?"

"Did I what?"

"Did you wecognise who did it?" Sam repeated.

"No, unfortunately not."

"I would wecommend you try and welax and wemain still. You are bleeding quite a lot. I will wing an ambulance."

"No, I don't want an ambulance. I will be fine," the man insisted.

"Are you Weggie?" Sam asked.

"Possibly," the bleeding man responded with a confused expression and then continued, "If you are the one I was supposed to give the package to, well whoever hit me has taken it."

"Oh, cwap," George said.

....

It was after midnight when George and Sam got to Sam's home.

"We are just going to have to tell them what happened," Sam said. "It's not your fault your contact got clobbered and the package stolen."

"I just hope they see it that way. I am not sure they are the forgiving sort," George replied.

"It will be fine you'll see. First thing in the morning we will go and see them. I will make up a sofa bed for you for tonight," Sam said reassuringly.

3.

"I have often wondered what happened to the money donated by people attending church and all those funds raised at church coffee mornings and the like," Sam said.

Sam and George were stood outside a pair of high, heavy looking, black metal gates. The sort of gates designed to withstand a long-term siege from a determined enemy, and they were locked. While being watched by a closed-circuit television camera positioned on top of one of the tall brick gate pillars, they had pressed an entry intercom button to announce their arrival, and they were patiently waiting for a response.

Suddenly a voice said,

"You're late George, we expected you last night. Who is that with you?"

"This is a good friend of mine, he…"

"Oh, never mind," the voice impatiently interrupted. "Come in before I grow so old that I can't remember Terry Wogan."

And with that the two gates slowly opened to reveal a very large house surrounded by manicured gardens. As Sam and George stepped through the entrance, seemingly out of nowhere two well dressed, very big men with two very vicious looking, barking dogs appeared.

"Follow us," one of the men said, while restraining his dog from tearing Sam's leg off.

"Nice dog," Sam said nervously. He and George looked at each other and did as they were told.

Sam and George were escorted around to the rear of the large house and across a garden terrace with an ornate fountain, to a pair of patio doors. One of the two dog handlers opened a patio door and indicated for Sam and George to enter. Exchanging slightly apprehensive glances, Sam and George again did as instructed. They entered a room filled with palm plants and soft music. In the centre of the room stood a very tall man, completely bald, he was dressed in a white t-shirt, loose fitting white trousers and sandals. He didn't look up or speak when Sam and George entered the room but continued to massage the man lying face down on the polished steel masseur's table in front of him. That man was the bishop, who was naked apart from a white towel over his middle.

"Now George, what do you have to tell me?" the bishop asked.

"Well, it's like this your excellency. Last night, as agreed, I went to collect the package from the man at the airfield with my friend Bertram. Unfortunately, however, when we got there the man, that is to say Reggie, had been assaulted by someone who Reggie said had also then taken the package. I am very sorry. I did my best, really, I did."

"Well, this is disturbing news, isn't it," the bishop said while indicating to the masseur to go a little higher.

"I am very sorry. I did my best," George repeated.

"Now calm yourself George, this isn't the Old Testament. If it were, I would have your nose cut off and nailed to the front door of the local vicarage."

"Thank you for not having my nose cut off," George replied, rather sheepishly.

"Well, it would also be rather messy and I have just had this floor polished. Tell me George, if you were me what would you in these circumstances say to you?"

"Erm, well let me think. I would say, thank you, George, I know you have done your best. It doesn't matter about the money you owe us, go home and eat a large number of your favourite pies?"

"No, I would never say that. Which is why you are not me."

While all of this was going on Sam was feeling increasingly awkward and as casually as he could found himself staring at the newly polished floor and shifting his weight from one foot to another. At the same time however, he could not help but wonder what was in the package George was to collect. Also, how a career in the church was nothing like what he had imagined.

"This is what you would say to you," the bishop said. "You and your friend here have got 24 hours to retrieve the package and return it to me. Otherwise, you will receive a visit from some of my flock carrying baseball bats. Then having visited you they will visit your sausage guzzling parents and extract what you owe from them. Have you got that?"

"Yes, your excellency."

"Now get out while I am still in a forgiving mood," the bishop said sternly.

Sam and George quickly left by the way they had come in and the high black metal gates closed behind them.

"What are we going to do Bertie? What are we going to do?"

"Now take it easy George, we will think of something."

"But I don't want to be beaten to a pulp by angry parishioners and my parents will go mad if they have to bail me out of another gambling debt."

"Whoever assaulted Reggie must have known of the package. A disused airfield is not the sort of place people would normally be casually wandering around and certainly not at that time of night. Let's see if we can talk to Reggie. He had a bad wound and although he didn't want me to call an ambulance, he may have gone to the local hospital to get it patched up. If he did then they may have a home address. We will start there."

....

The hospital car park was busy. It was also eye-wateringly expensive, so much so that they offered what they believed to be attractive credit terms for regular users. Unsurprisingly, there were numerous vehicles parked in an abandoned sort of way near the hospital and the streets which led to it.

"It makes as much sense as councils charging for the collection of unwanted household items and then expressing surprise at the amount of fly tipping. Which in turn not only spoils the environment but also costs twice as much to collect," George said, while watching an ambulance mount a kerb in order to get to the hospital's Accident and Emergency entrance.

Sam nodded knowingly.

As it happened a car park user was leaving his space just as Sam and George arrived, and after some bartering agreed to sell the time which remained on his parking ticket at the current rate minus five per cent – plus George's watch.

Entering the main hospital entrance, Sam and George approached the reception counter, where two very overweight women in very tight-fitting uniforms were in conversation.

"Well, I told her that she didn't know what she was talking about. I am the perfect weight for my height, I am just heavy boned. And my clothes appear too small because the dry cleaners keep shrinking them."

"And what did she say?"

"She didn't say anything. She just gave me a couple of diet plans."

"Were they any good?"

"They were perfect. When I came out of the bakers it was raining so I used them to cover my vanilla cheesecake."

"Good idea. By the way are you going to eat that last pie of yours?"

"Yes."

"Excuse me," Sam said interrupting, and checking whether he and George had become invisible.

"Yes, how can we help you," one of the receptionists said.

In a well-practised motion Sam very briefly showed an identity card, which, to anyone not looking too closely, might pass for a Police Identification card.

"We are looking for some information regarding a person who may have been treated at this hospital late last night."

"If it were last night, he would have been seen by Doctor Jones. There he is now," the receptionist pointed and then called out, "Doctor Jones, do you have a moment, these two Policemen would like a word."

After a hurried discussion, as it was the doctor's break, it seemed Reggie had indeed visited the hospital the night previous for treatment of his head wound. After what became a disturbingly lengthy search through hospital records, Sam and George were given Reggie's home address.

Leaving the hospital George whispered to Sam,

"Where did you get that Police Identification card?"

"Oh, that. I have had it years. I got it from Woolworths along with a whistle, a truncheon, a pair of hand cuffs and a toy policeman's helmet."

"Wow," George replied.

"People see what they want to see, and generally never ask questions," Sam said.

"What if they do? What if some person asked for a closer look at your identification card?"

"Then, I would do one of three things. I would pretend to faint. I would distract them somehow such as suddenly telling them to look out, or, I would run away."

"Interesting," George said, while giving his friend a strange look.

4.

83 Rachman Road was a flat above a bookmaker just off the town's High Street.

"There used to be a time when I couldn't walk past one of those without going in," George said indicating toward the betting shop window.

Sam didn't respond but simply knocked on the door of the flat causing some of the flaking green paint to fall off. They waited, but there was no response. Sam knocked again a little harder hurting his knuckles in the process.

"Looks like he isn't in," George said.

"Could be," Sam replied. "We will try again later"

As Sam and George began to walk away an upstairs window noisily opened and a voice shouted,

"Who is it? What do you want?"

Sam and George looked up to see a man dressed in a t shirt and with a bandaged head.

"It's us", George shouted, "we met last night at the abandoned airfield."

"Shhh" the man said loudly, "I will be right down."

Moments later Sam and George heard the sound of bolts being withdrawn on the other side of the door which then quickly opened.

"Come in, come in," he said hastily and when they had done so he checked outside to see if anyone was about. Sam and George ascended the dark narrow stairs to the landing and were ushered into a small living room.

"What are you doing here? What do you want? Reggie asked anxiously.

"We are trying to locate the package taken from you last night. You said you did not see the person who took it, but what about the person who asked you to deliver it. Who was that?" Sam asked.

"A stranger. A complete stranger to me, Reggie said, shrugging his shoulders. "I was in the pub just around the corner from here having a quiet drink and this person came over. Well, we got on talking and I told him I as an actor looking for work but not having much luck at the moment. He asked me if I would like to earn £500 and I said I would. Who wouldn't after all? But told him that I wasn't prepared to do anything illegal."

George interjected, "Have you been in any movies?"

"Yes," Reggie replied enthusiastically. "I played a dead person in the film *The Reluctant Cowboy*. I played "man sleeping in alleyway" in the film *The Gangster with a Speech Impediment*. Also, you may have seen the current tv advert for verruca cream. Well, that is my foot."

"Excellent," Sam said. "Now can we focus on the task in hand? This man, this stranger, what can you tell us about him?"

"Well, not a lot really. He was just an average bloke, average height, average build, no distinguishing features that I can recall. Just the sort of person you would meet in a pub, I suppose. He gave me a key to a changing room locker at the nearby leisure centre, number 56 I think, anyway he told me inside the locker I would find a parcel and that I should take this parcel to the disused airfield where I should hand it over to a person who would be there to collect it."

Sam turned to George. "We need to get to this leisure centre."

"Well, if it's all the same to you I am not really in the mood for any sort of sporting activity, and besides I haven't brought my kit."

"In order to find out anything about this locker," Sam explained.

"Oh, yes of course. Right behind you mate," George replied.

"Good luck with the movie career Reggie," Sam said, and he and George left.

....

The nearby leisure centre had the outward appearance of a post-world war Russian power plant. In fact, visually its only redeeming feature was its car park which unusually had spaces large enough to safely park a modern vehicle. Inside by contrast Sam and

George found a bright, airy space with lots of highly polished surfaces.

The high reception counter was adorned with numerous colourful posters publicising the many activities available at the centre, from badminton to do it yourself open heart surgery. A young woman, who was attractive in a brutal sort of a way, stood behind the counter and watched Sam and George approach. Sam momentarily produced and quickly closed his police identification card from Woolworths and said to the young woman,

"I would like to see the manager please."

The receptionist picked up the phone from the counter, pressed a single key and said,

"Simon, the Police are here to see you. Would you like me to show them through?"

Then, replacing the handset, she said,

"Follow me please."

Sam and George were shown down a chlorine-smelling corridor past the entrance to the swimming baths to a small office with a large calendar wall chart, and an equally large health and safety notice – the sort which the law demands are displayed but nobody ever reads.

"Good morning, my name is Simon, how may I help you?"

"We have reason to believe that one of your changing room lockers was recently used to store stolen goods," Sam said.

"Oh, my goodness" Simon replied in a concerned voice, "Which one?"

"We think it was locker 56."

"Let me call in my assistant manager Sheila, she looks after that side of things." Simon picked up his phone and asked Sheila to come to his office.

"Sheila, these are the police. They say some stolen goods may have been stored in one of our changing room lockers, number 56. Do you know anything about it?"

"That is the locker where the key went missing for a couple of days and then mysteriously turned back up again. When the key reappeared, I checked the locker and it was empty. I just assumed the key must have fallen to the floor and then later someone found it and put it back in the locker."

"I notice you operate a cctv system in the centre. Would it be possible to see it?"

"Certainly," Simon replied and he, Sheila, Sam and George went to Sheila's office where the cctv equipment was held. Incidentally Sheila's office also had an identical large calendar wall chart and equally large health and safety notice. The four of them began viewing the tapes. After a short while of watching the viewing screen Sheila gave a harrumphing noise.

"What is it?" Simon asked her.

"That's Ray Stobbs, he used to live beside my mother. I don't know what he is doing here after opening time. My mother use to say he spent most of his life in the pub. She also said that he has been convicted previously of petty theft and shoplifting. Probably to feed his drinking habit. Someone once said he was from a very well to do family who now don't want anything to do with him."

"And I see he is carrying a small package," George said.

"Probably a bottle of beer," Sheila responded sarcastically.

"You don't happen to know his address?" Sam asked.

"I certainly do," Sheila replied.

…………………..

Ray lived in an end terraced house in an old but pretty street. Pretty that is, apart from his front garden which had a post-apocalyptic appearance, with long grass growing through an abandoned shopping trolley and around discarded cardboard boxes disfigured by rain. Ray lived with his sausage dog, Spartacus, which for some reason had decided to adopt Ray. Ray was comfortable with this arrangement. He in turn was convinced the dog spoke several languages and, on some occasions, particularly in the middle of the night after a heavy drinking session would give Ray horse racing tips. Much to the annoyance of neighbours, for no apparent reason the dog barked incessantly.

The house next to Ray was empty and had been for some time. Even homeless families, having seen Ray's home and heard Spartacus, had refused the opportunity to live there.

Sam and George entered through a gap in a wire boundary fence presumably where a gate had once hung. They made their way up the badly cracked garden path doing their best to avoid the tall weeds and nettles growing through it. Sam knocked on the house front door which it seemed once had a centre glass panel but was now covered with a piece of hard board poorly nailed over it.

"Enter, the door is open," a well-spoken voice from within the house said over the noise of a barking dog.

Pushing the front door open Sam and George entered a small, sparsely furnished room.

"Good afternoon gentlemen, how may I be of service?" said a man standing up from his armchair and motioning to shake their hands. He was dressed in an old-fashioned pinstripe suit very much in need of a dry clean, an once light blue shirt with a fraying collar, and a crumpled looking but neatly knotted tie.

"Good afternoon," Sam said, shaking Ray's hand. George did the same. Then following some initial introductions Sam asked,

"We believe you have recently visited the town's leisure centre."

"No, not me, sir," Ray replied, "Why do you ask?"

"You haven't been to the local leisure centre?" Sam again asked.

"No, never set foot in the place since it was built. Awful looking place. Should be pulled down."

"Okay, let me start again. Less than an hour ago we looked at some cctv footage which showed you entering the local leisure centre last Tuesday at ten past two in the afternoon."

"Oh, yes, that's right, that was me, I popped in for a game of squash."

"No, you popped in to deposit a parcel in locker 56," Sam said.

"Who are you? What is going on? Are you the local constabulary?" Ray asked realising he had been found out.

"No, we are not with the Police, we are simply acting for a friend and need to retrieve the parcel you left," Sam said reassuringly.

"Look I don't want any trouble. I was experiencing a cash flow problem at the time and a man came up to me in the pub and offered me £500 if I would take this locket from his friend's house put it in a box he gave me, and deposit it in this changing room locker. He said it was a joke. His friend would be out and it was all in good innocent fun. Well, as I say I needed the money. So, I did it. I don't know what happened to the locket after that. I just left it in the locker and gave the locker key to the man in the pub and he gave me £500."

"This man in the pub," Sam said, "Who was he?"

"I don't know, I hadn't seen him before. He didn't give a name. He was just an average chap, average height, average build, the sort of chap you meet in a pub. He seemed pleasant enough, not one of those riff raff."

"Okay, what was the address he gave you? The address of his friend's house?" Sam asked.

"Good question. I have it written down somewhere," Ray said, fumbling through his jacket pockets. "Here it is, 18 Bowes Court. There are fields at the back of it. That is how I got in."

"We intend to knock on the front door," Sam replied.

"Oh well, each to his own," Ray said.

5.

"All of this over a locket?" George said, while inputting Bowes Street into his car's sat nav. "I wouldn't have thought the bishop would be interested in jewellery. It must be incredibly valuable."

"Possibly," Sam replied, clearly deep in thought.

Then pointing to the satnav screen in his car George said,

"I know where this is. In fact, near there is a very good Greek bistro called Zorba's if you fancy something to eat. My stomach has been growling ever since we left the leisure centre."

"Actually, I wouldn't mind something. But we dare not stay long. We mustn't forget the clock is ticking."

"Trust me Bertie this place does the best moussaka you have ever tasted. By the way the owner isn't actually called Zorba, it's Colin, but he thinks Zorba's adds a touch of authenticity. Just a word of warning though, try and avoid Colin's wife Sophia. It is said that she takes after her mother who emigrated back to Crete during the Second World War just so she could strangle Nazis."

"Thanks for the tip off," Sam replied, and off the car went.

....

The Mediterranean chalk blue painted window frames and doors made the bistro instantly recognisable as Greek.

"So, you have been here before?" Sam asked.

"Once or twice", George replied while opening the door to Zorba's.

Stepping inside the two were greeted with the scent of garlic and the sound of traditional bouzouki music. Then as they removed their coats a loud voice from across the large room shouted,

"George, how are you, good to see you again."

"Well, maybe three or four times," George said in a hushed voice.

A very large man dressed in rather tight-fitting white shirt and black trousers and with his arms open ready to embrace approached George.

"My friend, how are you? Do you want your usual table?"

"Yes please," George replied. "I am well and this is my good friend Bertie, how are you?"

"Busy, always busy. Welcome Bertie. Welcome to my bistro," Colin said laughing and vigorously shaking Sam's hand.

Sam and George were shown to a round table near a large rustic wine rack.

"Now tell me George," Colin said, "Is it your usual? Moussaka?"

"Yes, please," George replied excitedly.

"With extra aubergines and cheese?" Colin asked.

"Definitely," George responded.

"And for you, my friend?" Colin asked Sam.

"I will have the same please."

"I will tell my wife. You see, Bertie, my wife Sofia she does the cooking and I do the tasting," Colin laughed loudly, while resting his large hands on his much larger stomach which shook vigorously as he did so. He then made his way toward the kitchen lifting an empty bottle of wine from a table as he passed. When the door to the kitchen was opened a small woman with thick black curly hair came into view. Colin entered. Moments later he left to the very loud threatening voice of Sophia,

"And if you do that again I will stick a fork in your eye."

Colin quickly and very sensibly made himself scarce.

Looking about the bistro, Sam could see a large mural depicting a Mediterranean shoreline with brightly coloured fishing boats, and small white painted houses with terracotta roofs. The other walls were covered in dated framed posters of olives, lemon trees, and bottles of wine. Painted plates and religious icons hung precariously here and there and artificial vines grew up wooden trellis. The place wasn't busy but there were a number of customers occupying tables and seemingly enjoying a meal. Suddenly Sam was startled by one of the clientele and turned to George who was closely studying Zorba's menu.

"Don't look now," Sam whispered, "Over there in the corner, isn't that the man we saw earlier today giving the bishop a massage?"

"When can I look?" George whispered back while continuing to gaze at the menu.

"What?" Sam said.

"You said not to look now. I am asking you when can I look."

"It's just a figure of speech," Sam replied.

"Is it? Well, if it is, and I am not convinced that it is, I for one have never heard of it before."

"Okay. Is he or is he not the person we saw earlier?" Sam said, indicating as casually as he could toward the corner of the room with several unnatural sideway movements of his head.

"Yes, it is", George replied. "Do you think he has followed us here?"

"No."

"Why not?"

"Because he was here first," Sam replied.

"Good point. So, what are we going to do? We can still have our moussaka, can't we?"

"I can't see why not."

"Yes, might as well. Who do you think that person is he is with?" George asked.

"Goodness knows. I don't think I have ever seen him before."

"Whatever it is they are eating looks nice, doesn't it," George said assuredly.

Sam gave his friend a questioning look.

For those readers who are interested to know, the moussaka eaten by Sam and George was indeed very nice and fortunately, Colin did not get a fork stuck in his eye – well not on that particular day anyway.

6.

Bowes Court was a small cul-de-sac. The sort of place when you enter you can't help but feel at least one person is staring at you from behind a curtain. The sort of place where it is noted if you failed to change your car when the vehicle registration plate changed.

George drove slowly into the cul-de-sac past the twitching curtains, highly polished cars, and faded Neighbourhood Watch signs. He stopped outside number 18 and its neatly cut, geometrically perfect privet hedge.

"So, tell me once more, why is it we are here Bertie?"

"Well, firstly, if the locket is valuable, its rightful owner may well have taken a photograph of it for insurance purposes. If we can see that photograph then at least we will know exactly what it is we are looking for. And secondly, Ray said that he had been told by the person in the pub that the occupier of the house would be out and the property would be empty. So, I reckon there is a good chance that the person who lives here may well be acquainted in some way with the person who organised the theft. Whether they realise that or not is of course a different matter. I am also of the opinion that somewhere along the line there may well have been a double cross."

"I wish I had never asked," George replied.

"Don't worry, just follow my lead."

Sam and George got out of the car and made their way up the short path to the house. Sam rang the doorbell and reached for his Woolworth's police identification card. Moments later the door opened and a tall man in a police uniform stood before them.

"Er...good afternoon..." Sam said, a little taken aback but not so much that it prevented him from hurriedly pushing his identification card unopened back into the inside pocket of this jacket. "I wonder..." Then before he could utter another word George interrupted,

"It's Ben, isn't it? Benny Blamires from Whorlton Street. We used to play together as kids. If it isn't you then you have a double."

"Why yes, it is. Goodness me its George Davidson. How on earth are you and what are you doing knocking on my door after all these years? Please come in."

George introduced Sam and the three men went through and sat down in a large conservatory.

"So, tell me George, do your parents still have that pie factory? And I must ask because I recall you always were so proud of the fact; did you ever manage to beat your record of eating five pork pies in a minute?"

Recollections of fond memories of their early childhood continued for a short while until Sam reminded George of the time factor and maybe he should explain to his friend the reason for their visit.

"Yes, please do," Ben said.

"Okay," George said and took a deep breath, "I owe this guy some money and he says if I did an errand for him, he would forget about the money I owed."

"An errand?" Ben said.

"Yes, I was to collect a package from Reggie who would be at an abandoned airfield."

"An abandoned airfield," Ben said, raising his eyebrows.

"Anyway," George continued, "when Bertie and I got there Reggie had been attacked and the package taken. When we explained this to the bishop…"

"The bishop?" Ben interrupted.

"Yes, the bishop, that is the person I owe the money to. He said we had 24 hours to recover the parcel otherwise there would be serious repercussions."

"Serious repercussions?" Ben said.

Sam began looking around to see what was causing the echo.

"Yes, he was having a massage by THAT MAN STARING IN YOUR WINDOW!"

Ben turned in his chair and saw the tall bald man who George and Sam had also seen at Zorba's.

"Just a moment," Ben said and got up from his chair and opened the door to the conservatory to let his visitor in.

"May I introduce a colleague of mine. This is Joe, he works as an undercover police officer."

"Hello Joe, pleased to meet you again. I think," George said, and Sam nodded in agreement.

Ben sat back down and cleared his throat.

"The person you are referring to as the bishop you will be surprised to know is in fact my cousin. We have been estranged for a number of years; I am aware of his activities through intelligence that Joe is skilfully able to gather. I was aware of the plan to steal the locket, and it was Joe who took it from Reggie. I hope Reggie isn't badly hurt by the way, but we had to make it realistic."

"He is fine," Sam interjected.

Ben got up from his chair and went to a small desk from which he took out a locket.

"This is the locket my cousin is after," Ben said.

"Well, I'll be blowed", George said.

"But it is not the locket itself which he seeks, it is what he believes to be inside it. Years ago, my grandfather gave a locket to each of his two daughters and inside each I understand was a valuable stamp. I say I understand because I have never seen the stamps. In fact, when years ago, I asked my mother, who is now deceased, as to the stamp's whereabouts she said she did not know and believed it to have been lost some time ago. I don't know anything about the stamp from the other locket. The locket belonging to my aunt was lost in a small house fire and I assume the stamp must have been lost along with it. If it ever existed at all, frankly I am not sure they did. Possibly my cousin has it, who knows? Anyway, he clearly believes that this locket still contains a valuable stamp and he wants to get his hands on it. I am sure the locket itself is of no significance to him, he probably doesn't even know what it looks like."

"If he does not know what the locket looks like can we not present him with the box and a different locket inside it? That would then free George from his debt and the threat of being beaten to a pulp. Sorry George," Sam said, turning to his friend.

"Well, if you are game, I am," Ben said.

"Me too," George added, "Anything to prevent being beaten to a pulp."

7.

Fortunately, Sam and George were able to locate a small jeweller in town just before it closed for the day.

"Are you looking for anything in particular, sir?" the smartly dressed lady standing behind the glass display counter enquired.

"Well, actually yes," Sam replied searching for the photos on his mobile phone. "We would like a locket which looks like this one, but as cheap as possible please."

"I sense either love on a budget is in the air, or possibly you wish to make some sort of statement?" the lady responded with a smile.

"I think this might meet your requirements," she said showing Sam and George a particular locket. "This one retails at £99"

"Don't you have anything a little less.... well.... ostentatious?" Sam asked.

The assistant sighed.

"By which you mean cheaper?"

"Yes."

After a short search the shop assistant said hesitantly, "Well, this one may fulfil your requirements? It would certainly send a statement when the item turns green through oxidation, confirming the fact that the locket is not in fact real gold. This one is £39."

"That will do," George said.

The lady gave a wry smile and said,

"If you would like we can have it engraved? "You cheating bitch" springs to mind? Or, simply "I hope you die" is popular at the moment."

"No thank you, we don't want it engraved," George said.

"Would you like me to wrap it for you? We have three types of wrapping ranging from the quality you would expect to find hanging in a public toilet to our "Everything I have is

Yours" range which I suspect doesn't apply in this particular case."

"No thank you. It is not necessary to wrap it. We will just take it as it is," Sam said.

"If you like I could tie a brick to it if it is your intention to throw it?" the lady proffered.

"That sounds good", George said.

"No, thank you again. That won't be necessary," Sam replied.

....

Back at Bowes Court, Ben had found the box which Reggie was to give to George. Sam handed over the new locket and Ben put it into the box.

"There you are, ready for delivery," Ben said, handing the box to George.

"I do hope this works," George said. "I am concerned that if it doesn't the bishop will still come after me."

"Don't you worry yourself George, I can promise you that he won't come after you once you have delivered the parcel he wants so much."

George smiled a hopeful smile and he and Sam got into the car and left.

....

It was approaching 8 o clock in the evening when Sam and George pulled up outside the bishop's residence. They got out of their car and pressed the intercom on the gate pillar. A small but conspicuous camera whirred around and a voice said,

"Good evening, George, do you have my parcel?"

"I do, your excellency."

"Splendid, then please do come in," the voice said, and the high black metal gates slowly opened. Sam and George were guided to the main entrance of the house, whereupon the large front door was opened by a tall slim woman dressed in a traditional chambermaid's outfit.

"Please follow me," she said, in a strong French accent.

Sam and George were escorted down a spacious chandelier lit hallway, large paintings hung on the walls, they passed several large armchairs and two antique sideboards upon which stood a number of sizeable ornaments. Everything they could see didn't suggest opulence it shouted it and with a capital O.

They were shown into a room where they found the bishop sitting on a reclining chair. He was wearing a thick white robe and had a matching towel wrapped around his head. Another woman, this time dressed in a white tunic, was giving him a pedicure.

"Good evening, George and friend. I hope you have had a good day."

"Well actually…." George started. The bishop interrupted holding up his hand,

"Frankly, I am not really interested," he said.

"No, of course not," George replied submissively.

"Now, I understand you have my parcel. So, hand it over," the bishop said stretching out his hand.

George handed over the parcel.

"Thank you, my son. Now go away."

Sam and George turned and left as quickly as they dared without making it obvious that they wanted to run as fast as their legs would carry them. The tall slim woman dressed in the chambermaid's outfit closed the front door of the house behind them.

....

The car park of the Ship Inn was quite busy when Sam and George parked up.

"Well, that takes care of that," Sam said.

"I do hope so. I know it was my fault for running up the debt but I have learned my lesson and thankfully never gamble now. I just hope the bishop will let it go," George replied.

"Oh, I think he will".

"But how can you be sure?"

"Ben showed me a note which he put in the box with the locket, it read, There is no stamp so stop wasting your time. George is a good friend of mine who has upheld his part of the bargain. If you pursue him further, I will have our Vice section, call on you. Your loving cousin, Chief Superintendent Ben Blamires.

"Well, that should do it," George said, with relief.

"Fancy something to eat? My treat."

"Sounds good to me," Sam replied.

....

The following morning was bright and warm. Sam cycled to work humming an unrecognisable but pleasant tune. He felt good about himself. He had managed to help his friend George out of a jam and rekindled his friendship with him. Not only that, his secretary Barbara had decided to move on, and as a result he saw a rebirth of his business on a more professional footing. He began to envisage a marketing campaign, professional business cards, maybe tv advertising? He pedalled excitedly.

"Good morning, Barbara," Sam said as he breezed into his office. "Isn't it a beautiful day."

"Er yes," Barbara replied. "Actually, do you have a minute?" she asked.

"Of course, Barbara, anything for you."

"Well, I have been thinking. After all the nice things you said to me the other day, being hard to replace and all that, I realise that I can't leave you in the lurch, not after all of our time together, so I have decided to stay. But given how valuable I clearly am to the business, I was also thinking it's high time I had a pay rise. Shall we say 20%?"

The Casebook of Private Investigator Sam Sloane

Mind Games

1.

The room ceiling light flickered. Sam paid it no heed. As far as he was concerned bulb replacement fell within the domain of Do It Yourself and, if only in the interests of personal safety, he preferred to avoid such activity. As far as he was concerned people who claim to enjoy DIY were out of touch with reality and lived in a parallel universe. Sam was leaning motionless against his kitchen work bench, seemingly mesmerised by the sight and sound of his microwave oven as it cooked his lasagne ready meal. He was pleased to be home as it had been a day which he was happy to forget. It had started well enough; in fact, the morning had been quite productive. He had collected his shoes from the cobblers, had his ears syringed, and visited the Post Office for some foreign currency for his forthcoming holiday to Majorca – something which he was now very much looking forward to.

While he waited for his food to cook Sam reflected on how much pets can mean to their owners. His client Mrs Lawrence was proof of that. She had visited Sam at his office earlier that afternoon.

"Oh, Mr Sloane I do hope you can help me. It's my cat, Lambert, he has gone missing. He didn't come home for his lunch and it is so unlike him. It was his favourite, fresh Scottish salmon. He is normally so prompt, Mr Sloane. You could almost set your watch by the sound of the cat flap opening. I am concerned that something may have happened to him. Will you see if you can find him, please?"

"Well, I can certainly go look for him," Sam had replied, while smiling benevolently. "But it's only two o clock Mrs Lawrence. Are you sure you don't want to give him a little longer to return home? He may have just lost track of time and got caught up in deep conversation with some of his feline friends, discussing mouse killing techniques or such like. If it's his favourite meal then I wouldn't be surprised if you find he has returned home when you get there."

But Mrs Lawrence was insistent, so Sam went in search of Lambert. It was not long before he found him, or rather a group of school children saw him apparently stuck up a tree. It was at that point that Sam's day had taken a turn for the worst. Against his better judgement, and under a level of pressure from the children, he had climbed the tree which hadn't seemed that high when looking up at it from the ground. Much to the delight of the school children, and with the assistance of Sam's trouser leg which Lambert employed as a climbing net, the cat managed to get down from the tree and ran off without even a "thank you," no doubt soon to enjoy his fresh salmon. As for Sam, it was a very different matter. To him it seemed an age before the local fire brigade were able to attend. In the interim a large crowd had gathered below him many shouting unhelpful words of advice as to how he could get down. Sam, however, found himself frozen in fear clinging on to a lofty tree branch. Much to Sam's embarrassment when he was eventually returned over a fireman's shoulder to terra firma, the onlookers cheered and applauded loudly. The firemen were less appreciative, and had made that quite clear to Sam who in turn had been full of apology. As if to add insult to injury, on his way home Sam noticed a certain coolness on his right leg and realised that in climbing down from the tree Lambert had ripped his trousers.

....

Despite having watched the seconds count down on his microwave, he was startled when the bell sounded to indicate his meal was ready. He opened the microwave door and took the meal out, burning his fingers as he did so. He instinctively dropped the plastic tray containing his meal on to the kitchen bench and blew on his burning fingers. Then as quickly as he could he removed the cellophane cover, again burning himself in the process, and again blew on his fingers to cool them. With the aid of a tea towel, he lifted the plastic meal tray and slid the lasagne onto a large plate. With a grunt of satisfaction, Sam then made his way through to his living room where he switched on his television.

"Good evening, this is the late evening news. In the headlines tonight, television celebrity and self-publicist Sharon Demsey has tweeted that following her recent breast augmentation surgery she believes she now has the biggest breasts on tv. Sharon, who used to be married to game show host Zak Dimwhit, has recently launched a new lingerie and swimwear range and following her surgery has posted photographs of herself modelling the new range on her website. Earlier today our special celebrity correspondent, Bunty Sequin, spoke with Ms Demsey at her home in Essex.

"Now Sharon, I understand this is the third time you have undergone this type of surgery."

"That's right. I think it's important to like your body, particularly if like me you enjoy showing it off to anybody who is prepared to pay. And if that means an implant here and there then bring it on is what I say."

"So, are you saying the surgery is all about improving your personal self-esteem?"

"Undoubtedly, ...whatever that means. But it is also because I am prepared to do anything to be on tv. You know, some people say television celebrities have massive egos. Well, call them what you will, but I say if you have got them then show them off."

"The popular press and your publicity agent have gone on record saying that you believe yourself to be a role model for younger people. In which case, what message do you have for any younger viewers who may be watching tonight and who may well be influenced by what you say and what you do?"

"Don't take drugs, unless they are from a close friend, and get big boobs, they are great! Oh, and while I remember, don't forget to buy my latest book, it is an autobiography about me and it's all about my life, I am really looking forward to reading it, apparently, it's already a best seller. Also, check out my latest line in lingerie and swimwear. And don't listen to what other people are saying about it, it's not expensive rubbish."

"Well, there you have it," Bunty said, smiling. "Don't forget you heard it here first. Now back to you in the studio."

"Thanks Bunty. In other news tonight the Acid Bath Murderer has struck again, murdering his ninth victim, a school teacher from Liverpool. Also, scientists have advised that there is an eighty per cent chance that a meteorite the size of France will collide with the Earth in the next 48 hours. That's all from us for now. The latest information on your local weather is available by looking out of your window. I hope you enjoy the rest of your evening. Goodnight."

Sam switched his television off and reflected for a moment. If the world really was coming to an end, he needn't have bothered getting his shoes heeled. And what was he going to do with the euros he had just bought from the Post Office? He concluded that it just wasn't his day. He looked down at his unappetising lasagne. He thought the last time he had seen anything so runny he had drunk it through a straw. He bent over to reach for his glass of milk and his meal slipped off the plate and onto the carpet. Sam looked sorrowfully down at the puddle of pasta and wondered what Lambert was having for his supper. Probably he thought, beef bourguignon served with a saucer of a cheeky chardonnay. He decided the best thing he could do was to go to bed.

As Sam climbed what seemed that night to be a much longer staircase with much higher stairs his mobile phone rang.

"Hello."

There was no response.

"Hello," Sam said again only a little louder.

Again, there was no response other than a short squealing noise. Rather like the sound Sam imagined you might get if you kicked a guinea pig into an electric fan.

2.

Sam woke with a jolt. Opening his eyes, he struggled to focus. At least he thought he did. The problem as he saw it was that he did not appear to be where he thought he should be: in bed, in his bedroom and in his house. As initial impressions go, what he saw looked like a dark back alley. His first thought was that he was dreaming. He decided the best thing to do was to turn over, pull up his duvet and go back to sleep. But in doing so he bumped his head against a large steel wheelie bin. His second realisation was that he was wet, very wet, and looking down he realised he was lying in a small puddle. He also noticed that it appeared to be raining. Totally bewildered and moving only very slowly he gently guided his thought process through several small steps. He was outside, in a dark alley, now sitting in a puddle of rain, and leaning against an evil smelling wheelie bin. What on earth was going on? What was he doing there? And what had happened to his bedroom? Suddenly he remembered the meteorite. The scientists had got it wrong he thought, it wasn't coming in 48 hours, it had arrived much sooner, it had collided with the Earth while he was asleep in bed and somehow, he had ended up outside in this alleyway. But how was it he was again wearing the clothes he had worn the previous day when he had got stuck up a tree? He decided to come back to that.

Sam examined his arms and legs to check he wasn't hurt. He appeared to be unharmed. He pushed at the large wheelie bin to steady himself as he stood up. There was a groan from the other side of the bin where Sam discovered a dishevelled looking man lying against it.

"Are you okay?" Sam asked.

"What?" the other man groggily replied.

"I asked if you are alright."

"What is it? What do you want?" the man grumbled.

"It seems the meteorite has hit the planet sooner than expected," Sam said.

"What on earth are you talking about?"

"The meteorite," Sam said.

"I don't suppose you will be prepared to share whatever it is you have been drinking with me, would you?"

"I haven't been drinking," Sam said, affronted. "I don't mind telling you, I wish I had." Sam looked about, and as the dishevelled looking man appeared to be making no attempt to get up Sam said, "I tell you what, you stay here and I will go and check to see if I can find out what has happened. Then I will come back and let you know. Okay?"

"Suits me," the man replied and closed his eyes.

Sam made his way to the end of the alley where there was a tall wooden gate which he opened. To his surprise he found he was on his local high street. He checked his watch; it was three o'clock in the morning. A milk float went by, followed soon after by a baker's van. Sam turned towards the man still lying by the wheelie bin,

"Forget what I said," he shouted.

"I already have," the man replied and went back to sleep, cuddling a half empty bottle of cider.

Rather than try and order a taxi at that time of the morning, Sam decided to walk as fast as he could back to his home. As he did so he tried to make sense of what had happened. He was able to rule out the effects of alcohol because, as he had shared with the man in the alley, he hadn't had a drink. Could someone have surreptitiously given him drugs? He couldn't see when. Was this all just a dream? It certainly felt real, he thought, watching the rain run down his jacket. By the time he reached the front door of his home his head was still spinning, and unfortunately the only somewhat dubious conclusion he had come to was that he had somehow been abducted by aliens, who he knew from past experience to be out there. But why would they leave him in the alley?

Sam let himself in and went through to his living room, where he saw the pool of lasagne still on the carpet. Suddenly he thought, could it be that the ready meal was so out of date that it had affected his consciousness and as a result he had gone out into the rain? He knew he was grasping at straws but he would certainly prefer this to be the case rather than having been abducted by aliens. Rummaging through his kitchen bin he found the lasagne box. Sadly, he also found that it was well within date. Sam remained totally mystified. What had happened? Looking at his watch he realised that it would be dawn soon, so rather than go to bed, he decided to shower, change his clothes, and have an early morning coffee. Maybe then he would be able to think more clearly and it would all come back to him.

It was mid-morning and having cleared up the lasagne as best he could, Sam sat at his kitchen table drinking his coffee and shaking his head in bewilderment. He jumped with surprise when he suddenly heard a loud knock at his front door. Opening the door, he found two tall police officers standing there.

"Good morning, sir. Are you Bertram Edgeware, also known as Sam Sloane?"

"Yes, that's right, how can I help you?"

"Would you tell us where you were last night sir?"

"Actually, it's funny you should ask that question. I am not sure. All I can recall is that I woke up in an alleyway at about 3.00am and then I walked home."

"So, you don't remember visiting Hartigans the jewellers?"

"No, I don't."

"Bertram Edgeware, I am arresting you for breaking into Hartigans Jewellery store and stealing a number of valuable items from that store. You do not have to say anything. But it may harm your defence if you do not mention when questioned something that you later rely on in Court. Anything you do say may be given in evidence."

"I don't understand, I didn't break into Hartigans I don't even like the place, frankly I find the staff there to be rude and very unhelpful," Sam said.

"Please get into the back of our car, sir. We need to take you to the station for further questioning."

....

If you told anyone that the town's police station had won a design award when it was constructed in the late 1950's, that person would either think you were joking, or you had to be mistaken, or the judging panel at that time were taking drugs or were being blackmailed. It had the outward appearance of a Cold War fallout shelter to be used in the event of a nuclear attack. At the time of its construction the story around the town was that the architect's brother, who coincidentally owned a cement business, had misread the concrete tonnage order and produced ten times the amount required. A family dispute had resulted and a hasty redesign was required. In order to quash any rumour of wrong doing, the brother was somehow able to ensure an award for the building was forthcoming and family relations were thereby restored. Anyway, like it or not, there the award-winning building was, and no doubt there it would stay for some time to come. The police car containing Sam pulled up outside, the three occupants got out and Sam was escorted to the Custody Officer who was sitting at her desk in the main entrance to the station.

"Hello, hello, hello," she said, nodding to each of them in turn. "Sorry, I couldn't resist that."

Sam failed to see the humour.

"Oh, come on give me a smile," the Custody Officer said while completing the arrest form and indicating to Sam to empty his pockets. "Prison isn't so bad. So, you will probably get regularly beaten to a pulp, be abused in ways I would rather not mention and when you are eventually released, assuming you survive of course, you will be stigmatised for the rest of your life. But you will get used to it. You will have to," she said laughing.

Sam's eyes widened with the sudden realisation of his situation. Then before he could again plead his innocence another officer led him away to a side room, where he was asked to sit down at a small table. The officer escorting him also sat down.

"Now, Bertram, I am Sergeant Binks and we are going to have a little chat, but before we do, I am required to tell you that you have the right to free and independent legal advice and you have the right to tell someone where you are."

"But I haven't done anything wrong. So why would I want to see or contact anyone else?"

"Okay, well maybe if I show you this cctv footage first," the officer replied, and pressed a button on a remote control he had picked up from the table.

The small screen in front of them showed a brick coming through a large glass door and a person entering the shop and filling a bag with assorted watches and jewellery. It seemed clear from the cctv footage that the person in the shop was Sam who sat open mouthed as he watched the screen.

"Okay, that person looks like me," Sam admitted, "but it couldn't be me. I don't rob shops."

"Well, a prosecuting lawyer may disagree with you. Not only that, the staff at the shop recognised you from the cctv footage. They said you had recently been a troublesome customer."

"I only wanted a battery for my watch."

"Ah, so you admit it," Sergeant Binks interrupted, and before Sam could respond added, "Here is cctv footage from a similar event several days previous showing a robbery at the Market Cross jewellers."

Sergeant Binks again played some recorded footage.

"That isn't me," Sam blurted.

"Isn't it?" the officer replied, staring closely at the screen and then at Sam.

"No that's…"

"That's who?" Sergeant Binks asked.

"It's not me that's all. And I would like to make that phone call now please," Sam said.

Although he was not sure how his news of being under arrest would be received, he decided to ring his parents. His call was answered by their butler, James.

"Good morning, the Edgeware residence."

"Good morning, James, it's me," Sam said.

"Good morning, sir. I trust you are well."

"Actually, no I am not. I have been arrested and am being held at the local police station."

"I am distressed to hear that sir. How may I be of service?"

"Is my father there?"

"Lord Edgeware is currently in the garden sir, attempting to shoot some ramblers who have strayed onto his land. Would you like me to pass on a message while he is reloading?"

"Just mention my situation if you would, and ask him if he is able to help."

"Certainly sir, will that be all, sir?"

"Yes, thank you James."

Sam handed the phone back to the sergeant who asked,

"Would you like us to contact a legal advisor to represent you?"

"I think you'd better," Sam replied. Sergeant Binks made the necessary call.

Sam and the officer then sat silently as they waited. Then after about forty minutes the sergeant's phone rang.

"Oh, good morning, sir.... yes sir.... yes sir.... shows him clearly on the cctv footage.... his finger prints and DNA on the brick that broke the window and, in the jewellers,.... recognised by staff at the shop....no sir.... yes sir.... of course, sir.... right away sir.... thank you, sir."

The officer put his phone back in his jacket pocket, turned to Sam and with a grimace said in a begrudging tone,

"I have decided to release you without charge for the moment but remember this, I will be watching you. Don't you think of disappearing off anywhere soon. And stay away from jewellers' shops."

"Oh, right," Sam said rather surprised. "Thank you very much. So, I can go now?"

"Yes, off you go."

3.

It was now late morning, and leaving the police station Sam knew exactly where he was going. He was going to the home of Simon Day. Simon was the assistant curate of St. Benedict's church and, as Sam had realised from the cctv footage shown to him at the police station, the person who had robbed the Market Cross jeweller's store.

The assistant curate, a softly-spoken person, lived with his widowed mother, Janet, in an attractive-looking bungalow in Rosamand Terrace. Janet was a petite woman who exuded warmth and understanding. You wouldn't be surprised to see a blue bird sitting on her shoulder or her image on a get-well-soon card. She had silver grey hair which she kept in a bun, and wore pink rimmed spectacles which hung on a string around her neck. In those times when Sam had met her, she had always been wrapped in what seemed to be an oversized kitchen apron covered in flour. So much flour in fact that when she moved, she left a cloud of powder behind her.

Sam had met Simon about six months previous. Simon had sought Sam's help following a break-in at St Benedict's, for which Simon felt responsible. Unfortunately, he had inadvertently left the church unlocked one night and someone, clearly not a God-fearing person, had seized the opportunity to help themselves to the brassware. Needless to say, the news was not well received by the Parochial Church Council.

Thankfully the scrap metal dealer known locally as Big Don, who had subsequently been offered the religious artefacts in exchange for a digital car radio, contacted the police soon thereafter and the brassware was returned to the church. Big Don clearly wanted to demonstrate to the police that despite rumours to the contrary, he was in fact an upstanding citizen. Sadly, this was brought into question, and not for the first time, when two hundred state-of-the-art mobile phones missing from a local warehouse were later discovered in the boot of his BMW.

Sam knocked at the door of the bungalow and it was soon opened by Janet, who smiled through a cloud of flour.

"Oh, Mr Sloane, how fortunate it is that you should call. I was hoping to see you. Please come in."

Simon was out and his mother took the opportunity to share with Sam her concerns regarding her son's recent behaviour. How late one night having heard a noise she had got out of bed to find the front door of the bungalow wide open, and no sign of Simon. And how early the following morning the paper boy, when he saw Janet, had said he had just seen Simon apparently asleep next to a post box at the end of the street. Naturally Janet was concerned and had rushed out to see her son who by then was waking up. Simon, although in a confused state, was adamant that he had no idea how he had ended up there. Then today her son had suddenly started wearing a disguise.

"What do you think, Mr Sloane? It all seems so very unlike Simon. I am not sure what to do. Will you have a chat with him?"

"Of course, I will Mrs Day. In fact, as coincidence would have it that is exactly the reason why I called by, to have a chat."

Just at that moment there was the sound of the front door closing and Simon entered the room wearing a beret and false beard, both of which he quickly removed and pushed with some embarrassment into his coat pocket. Janet left the room to make some tea and check on her Victoria sponge cake.

"Hello Simon, I imagine you must be wondering why I have popped around to see you?"

In the hushed conversation which followed, Sam shared how and why he had been arrested and how he had also seen the cctv footage of Simon breaking into the Market Cross jewellers.

"I know it was me but it wasn't me, if you understand what I mean," Simon said.

"But how do you know it was you who did the deed?" Sam asked.

"Because the cctv footage was shown on Crimestoppers early this morning. That is why I am wearing this terrible disguise when I go out."

"Where have you been?" Sam asked.

"You're not going to believe this, but I have just been to visit one of my parishioners, a truly heavenly soul, but sadly absolutely distraught and wracked with guilt. It seems a week or so ago, very early one morning she woke up in her back garden to find that her handbag which she had with her was stuffed with fifty-pound notes. She swears she has no idea where the money came from, or how she came to wake up in her back garden. She feels so bad she has not been able to leave her house since. Not even with a beret and false beard which I offered to loan her."

"This is becoming very intriguing. Three normally law-abiding individuals each carry out a robbery of sorts and yet none of us can remember anything about it. There must be some connection, some common denominator somewhere. Tell me if you would, what did you do in the twenty-four hours before the jeweller's robbery?" Sam asked.

"Let me see," Simon said thoughtfully. "Ah, yes, on that particular day I had to meet an electrician at the church. St Benedict's really needs a rewire, I don't know how many times I have had an electric shock from the plug sockets. Anyway, I must have remained there most of the day doing various ecclesiastical tasks. Then when the electrician had finished, I came straight home to work on the church's books of accounts. I finished those late in the evening and went to bed early. That's right because I remember being awoken by my mobile phone ringing. Although strangely when I answered it there was no one there. All I heard was a loud screeching noise, rather like an old-fashioned fax machine. I assumed it must have been some sort of technical fault. Then next thing I knew was my mother waking me up next to a post box of all places."

"That was the same for me," Sam said excitedly.

"You woke up next to a post box?" Simon said.

"No, the loud screeching noise down my phone and then no subsequent recollection.

You need to speak again to your distraught parishioner and find out if she experienced the same thing. I would appreciate it if you would let me know as soon as possible. I have a hunch that this could be important."

....

It was mid-afternoon and Sam was back at his office marvelling at the possibilities afforded by a piece of surveillance equipment he had been able to acquire from a friend of a friend of a friend, who worked on the basis of no questions asked and cash only sales. It was a listening device which enabled the user to eavesdrop into conversations up to fifty yards away, even through a closed window. The problem however was that the instructions were in Russian, and no matter how loudly Sam spoke the words he tried to pronounce, he didn't understand a single one of them. Sam's phone rang, it was Simon.

"Hello Sam, apologies for not getting back to you sooner but I have only just been able to speak to my parishioner. I am delighted to say, thank God, that she has found the inner strength to leave her house. Apparently, she had been into town to pick up her new hearing aid. Anyway, you will be pleased to know that she does recall receiving a call similar to the one we received on the night of her as yet unknown experience."

"That is good news," Sam responded.

"Oh, the other thing which I neglected to mention when we spoke earlier and I don't know if it is important, but before I met the electrician at the church, I had a hearing test. And, coincidentally it was with the same audiologist as my parishioner, a Mr Foster, he is based at the opticians, Alexanders, the one on the High Street."

"That is very interesting, as that is the same person I visited on the morning of my unfortunate experience," Sam replied, in a slow and thoughtful tone.

4.

Sam sat drumming his fingers on his office desk. His facial expression portrayed a man agonising over something. What was going on? he thought. What was he missing? What had happened to the jewellery from the two shop robberies? Was there some connection with the audiologist - at that moment it appeared to be the only thing linking Simon, himself and the pious parishioner. How could he find out? Did any of this matter if the Earth was on a collision course with a meteorite the size of France? Just then his office door opened, it was his secretary, Barbara, who gave him a worried look as she placed a cup of coffee down in front of him on his desk.

"If you don't mind me saying so, you don't seem your usual self Mr Sloane. Is everything all right?"

"Actually, no Barbara, it isn't. I was arrested this morning for a crime which I didn't commit. Well, I suppose I may have committed it but I didn't, if you know what I mean."

"You mean you changed your mind halfway through committing the crime and so didn't fully carry it out."

"No, I mean I was recorded on cctv carrying out the crime I am accused of, but I don't remember doing it."

"Oh, I see, don't tell me you stole a load of beer, got hammered and don't remember what you did. That has happened to me before. If you have a bad head, I have some pain killers in my bag. They are very good, I got them off a man in the park. He said he was a doctor."

"No, I didn't steal a load of beer as you put it. It seems that I broke into a jewellery store."

"Wow, did you get anything nice because I am looking for a bracelet to match this necklace I am wearing, but can't find one anywhere. Well, not at the right price."

"That is part of the problem. I don't know where the jewellery I am accused of stealing is either," Sam replied.

"Wow, you must have had a lot to drink."

"I hadn't been drinking," Sam stressed in exasperation. "Why does everyone assume that?"

"What are you saying, you were hypnotised into doing it? Because I was hypnotised once and I was made to do all sorts of things. Then they put me into the boot of an old car and took me over the border into North Korea."

"What?" Sam said astonished. "I had no idea. What happened?"

"Well, they took me to this large building with no windows and there they asked me all sorts of strange questions. All about the sudden collapse of a government."

"And?" Sam said, after an unexpected silence.

"Oh, well after a few days they put me on a plane and sent me home. They even gave me a motorcycle escort to ensure I didn't miss the plane, which I thought was nice of them. But between you and me I wouldn't want to go back there again. The food was terrible and that car boot they put me in smelled of paint. I hate the smell of paint."

"You know I think you could be on to something," Sam said.

"You're thinking of having the office decorated?"

"No, I think I may well have been hypnotised somehow. Something tells me that I need to pay another visit to that audiologist."

"Why? Have your ears filled up with wax again?" Barbara said in a loud voice.

....

It was now late afternoon and Sam thought if he was quick, he would probably still manage to catch the audiologist at his place of work, namely at the shop unit he shared with Alexanders the opticians. He pulled on his rain coat and set off at a pace. As he neared the bus stop, a bus pulled up and Sam ran to it. Relieved and slightly out of breath having caught it, he jumped on board and was confronted with a triple XL driver who must have been shoehorned behind the vehicle's driving wheel. Her demeanour and bristled hairstyle reminded Sam of a female Russian shot putter he had once encountered, who used to shave the palms of her hands.

"Alexanders opticians please," Sam said.

"We stop at the bottom of the High Street and the top of the High Street. Which stop do you want?" the driver said while pulling a face which suggested she was having a problem with trapped wind.

"Oh, whichever one is nearest Alexanders?"

"That would be the top of the High Street. That will cost you £2.40."

The bus was busy with only a few vacant seats. Sam sat down next to an elderly looking lady holding tightly onto a large straw shopping bag resting on her lap. She smiled at Sam.

"Are you going for your flu jab?" she asked.

"No, not today. I am just popping into town to do some errands," Sam replied.

"We are all going for our flu jab."

Sam smiled and looked about him and noticed everyone else on the bus also appeared to be of an age where comfort was more important than speed. They all smiled at him.

"Can be a terrible thing the flu," Sam said to his seat companion, trying to make polite conversation.

"Oh, I have had a lot worse. I keep a picture of flu virus in a heart shaped frame next to my bed. I have had Ebola, diphtheria, smallpox, leprosy twice. And I died when I caught the bubonic plague."

Sam turned and gave her a look of disbelief.

"Well, I got better," she said.

Before Sam had the opportunity to investigate whether there was a current public transport passenger exchange scheme with hell, the bus arrived at his stop and he got off.

"Bye," Sam said and smiled and waved. Everyone on the bus except the bus driver, smiled and waved and shouted, "bye." While the doors to the bus were open the bus driver took the opportunity to relieve some of her abdomen pains.

....

Entering Alexanders Opticians Sam managed to get the attention of one of the members of staff, who appeared to be pre occupied checking her make-up in one of the many wall mirrors.

"I know it is late but would it be possible to see Mr Foster, the audiologist?" Sam asked.

"I am sorry but he has already left for the day."

"Oh, that is unfortunate. I have an urgent message for him. Do you happen to have his home address?"

"I am very sorry but I am not allowed to give out that information. If you like I could try and contact him on his mobile phone and give him your message?"

"The message I have is rather personal and I would get into trouble if I gave it to anyone but him directly. Tell you what, if you give me his mobile number, I will ring him with the message. As I say it is rather urgent. Some might say a matter of life and death."

"Well, if it is that important and that urgent, I am sure it will be fine. You don't look like a criminal to me," the young member of staff said laughing, and rechecked her make-up in the mirror.

Sam smiled, thanked her for her trust, albeit arguably misplaced on this particular occasion, and left the opticians with the audiologist's mobile number. He now hurried to see an associate of his who was called Kevin but was referred to by the few people who knew him as Eric. Nobody seemed to know why he was called Eric, not even Kevin but he didn't seem to care, it was not important to him. As far as he was concerned, he had bigger things on his mind. However, before he got to Eric's den Sam had to pay a visit to the local bakers.

5.

Just as it is sometimes blatantly obvious when some people are not very good at certain things, such as Do it Yourself, parking a car or running a country, it is also often readily recognised when some people have an obvious natural talent. Eric (also known as Kevin) had a natural talent with information technology.

Eric lived alone in a two-storey Victorian town house, where he spent most of his time in the basement logged in to his various computer equipment. Eric wasn't anti-social, but he was an impatient sole who quickly tired of "thick people" and so preferred to avoid them.

Sam rang the house door bell and an automated message played:

"If you are delivering a parcel just leave it on the door step, I will pick it up. If you need to speak to me, write it down and post your message through the letterbox, I will get back to you. If it is you mother, sorry I have not visited in a while I promise I will do so soon."

Sam opened the letterbox and shouted,

"It's me Eric, Sam, I need to see you rather urgently. I have brought some of those ginger nut biscuits I know you like."

The front door automatically unlocked and opened. Sam entered and made his way down to the basement where he guessed Eric would be. He was right.

"Hello Eric, how have you been?"

Eric sat at a large wooden table upon which stood four substantial computer monitors, several key boards, numerous electric cables, and various other pieces of technical equipment unrecognisable to anyone who did not have an in-depth knowledge and understanding of information technology. The basement itself was brilliantly lit and crammed with what could only be described as works in progress.

"I am good thanks Sam. I am currently doing some work for NASA on cybernetics and artificial intelligence. Fascinating stuff."

"What about this big meteorite which they say is going to hit the earth sometime soon?" Sam asked.

"Don't you worry yourself about that, it's just the usual media hype. Firstly, it is nowhere near the size of France which I understand some people are claiming, and secondly it will miss the earth by at least 7,000 miles. Do you want to see it?"

"Why yes, but how?" Sam asked, looking about for a telescope.

"Oh, easy really. I just lock onto one of the space satellites. A Russian one actually but don't tell them that. They can be a bit funny about it."

Eric tapped on one of his keyboards and within seconds the meteorite came up on one of his large monitors.

"Wow, that's amazing," Sam said.

"There you are, totally harmless. If you ask me, they should fire some of these so-called journalists off into space. They can be so irresponsible. I am surprised some of them haven't reported a sighting of three green men each dressed as Elvis Presley surfing the meteorite across the heavens. Anyway, enough of that," Eric said. "What is this urgent issue you have; it wasn't the meteorite was it?"

"No, it wasn't that. I didn't believe any of that rubbish about it hitting the earth. Size of France – pah. Utter garbage. No, actually it is more of a personal matter that I would appreciate your help with. I have someone's mobile phone number and I would like to know what their home address is. Would you be able to find that out for me?"

"Knowing you as I do, I am sure there will be a perfectly good reason for your request, so I won't pry. Let me have the number."

Seconds later Eric announced,

"Jason Foster, 14 Sycamore Street, not far from here actually. Nice looking house, big shed, I could use a garden shed like that. He is not there at the moment though. He is visiting the town's leisure centre."

"How do you know that?"

"His mobile phone signal. In fact, I can also tell you that there is currently nobody at home at 14 Sycamore Street. See...." Eric said while pointing at one of his computer screens, "no heat signs at the house, other than a cat or a very large mouse."

"That is amazing," Sam said.

"Ah, not really, you just have to know what you are doing," Eric said dismissively.

"That's great Eric thanks. I really appreciate it. Now I must dash. Oh, don't let me forget to leave your ginger nut biscuits. You have earned them. Bye for now."

"At least you pay quicker than MI5. I will enjoy these later with a cup of coffee," Eric shouted, as Sam hurried up the basement stairs and out of the house.

....

Sam soon found that speed walking in uncomfortable shoes can form a distraction when you are trying to formulate a plan of action. If Jason Foster had been hypnotising people to rob jewellery stores and goodness knows what else, Sam thought he was unlikely to admit it. Unless of course he had a sudden pang of guilt. At best Sam hoped his questioning may prompt Jason into some form of action which hopefully would not be in any way detrimental to Sam's health. But prior to that and assuming Jason had not returned home by the time Sam got there, he planned to have a look around to see if he could uncover anything out of the ordinary, but at this stage he was not sure what.

14 Sycamore Street was indeed an attractive suburban home, surrounded much to the immediate neighbour's dismay, however, by a high unkept hedge. In order to check that the house was still empty when he arrived, Sam rang the front door bell. Having had no response, and hidden by the high hedge, he made his way to the rear of the property. Sam peered in through the picture windows but saw little through the dark coloured louvre blinds. He therefore made his way to the unusually large garden shed, where he found the windows blanked over with sheets of paper. The door to the shed was padlocked, but as luck would have it the owner had neglected to remove the key. Sam quickly entered. The walls and ceiling of the shed had been heavily insulated, there was a

small table upon which sat some electrical equipment, a swivel office chair, and an assortment of old tea chests or packing boxes, the sort that people used to employ when moving house. It was clear that this was much more than a garden shed. It was well ordered and clean. Not somewhere you would keep garden tools or your dead wife with a surprised look on her face neatly chopped up in a chest freezer.

Sam examined the electrical equipment on the table and found what appeared to be the on/off button. About to press it, he heard the sound of a car door closing. Rather than risk being caught leaving the shed he crouched down behind some of the stacked tea chests. A moment later the door to the shed opened. Through a crack between the boxes Sam could see it was Jason Foster. He was carrying a metal box which he placed on the small table and as he did so his mobile phone rang,

"Jason Foster.... yes.... yes.... of course, I appreciate that.... I have it with me now.... eleven thirty tonight at Dalby's Cotton Mill, I will be there. Goodbye."

Jason replaced his phone back in his jacket pocket. He then gave the equipment on the table a thoughtful look and pressed the on/off button. The equipment played the same sound Sam had heard on his mobile phone the night he robbed Hartigan's the jewellers. Jason smiled to himself, switched the equipment off, gave it a light tap of appreciation, picked up the metal box and left the shed.

There was now no doubt in Sam's mind that Jason Foster was indeed behind the robberies using some form of mind control. But what was going to happen at Dalby's Cotton Mill later that night? Was the person Jason had been talking to on his mobile phone part of a larger illegal operation? Sam decided rather than confront Jason now he would go to the old cotton mill that night.

6.

Built in the early nineteenth century, in those dark days before cosmetic implants, fast food outlets and elasticated waist bands, Dalby's Cotton Mill, once a hive of activity, now stood empty and quiet.

According to a diary diligently kept by a local parson of that time, Sir Edward Dalby, the original owner of the mill, drank heavily and regularly dressed up in women's underwear, while his wife, Brenda, considered to be the brains behind the business, was an ardent cat lover and frequently ate small children for breakfast. This in turn served to encourage the mill's largely child labour force to work especially hard and therefore be as indispensable as possible.

Despite the passage of time, tales continued to be shared about the "goings on" at the old mill. How in days gone by employees could be crucified for being a minute late for work or forced to wrestle the owner's fourteen-foot Nile crocodile. How Brenda Dalby would regularly threaten to select and burn certain employees if production fell. And how to this day ghosts of ex-employees still roamed the mill and how lights had been seen from the mill despite it being empty and boarded up.

Sam's mind however was focused on the here and now. It seemed to him that he had been forced by an unscrupulous person to carry out a crime, a crime which otherwise he would not have dreamed of committing and there was no way he was going to be punished for it if he could help it.

....

Across the other side of town in the back garden of a three-bedroomed semi-detached house, an off-duty police officer was in his greenhouse tending his tomato plants and mumbling to himself. "What do they know? They have been too long in the job that's their problem. They now spend too much time ensuring political correctness and avoiding accusations of harassment and discrimination rather than fighting crime. No wonder people are losing faith in the police. It was an open and shut pinch. What more solid evidence did he expect?"

Just then the officer's mobile phone rang,

"Yes…. he said what? What's an audiologist when it's washed?. mind games?....where?....at eleven thirty….okay, but it better not be a wild goose chase, it's my darts night."

…………………..

Dalby's mill stood about a mile outside of town. Sam decided to walk the distance along a little used footpath. It was dark but it was dry and mild, and other than the odd rabbit which darted across his path nothing else appeared to stir. The only sound he heard was that of the long grass as it brushed against his recently cobbled shoes. After a short while the dark outline of the mill came into view. Sam instinctively slowed his pace as he checked about for any activity. There was none and then suddenly a voice said,

"Now then Bertram, I thought you would come this way."

Sam jumped.

"Oh, Sergeant Binks, you gave me quite a start. Thank you for coming. Hopefully I will be able to prove to you who and what is behind these jewel robberies."

"Hopefully? You had better. I am missing my darts night and we are in the quarter finals."

"All I know is that whatever it is that is happening, is happening at Dalby's mill tonight at eleven thirty."

"Okay, let's go and take a shufty," Sergeant Binks said, and the two of them cautiously made their way to the mill. As they approached, they heard some dull sounds and could see a dim light, both of which appeared to come from a lower floor of the mill, a basement of some sort. Sergeant Binks and Sam slowly descended the stone stairs and as they did so the sound grew louder and the light brighter. At the bottom of the stairs, they turned right and were immediately confronted by a tall man dressed in a long black hooded cloak, who said abruptly,

"Who are you?"

"We are invited guests," Sergeant Binks blurted.

"Really?" the hooded man said in a voice which suggested disbelief and the serious threat of unrestrained and well-practiced violence soon to follow.

"Yes," Sam responded.

"Are you sure?" the hooded man pressed with a growl.

"Definitely," Sergeant Binks replied.

"Oh well you had better go in then," the hooded man said and pointed, "and if you wouldn't mind standing over there and be quiet, he is about to arrive."

"Smashing," Sam said, and immediately wished he hadn't. Sergeant Binks gave him a disapproving look and ushered him to move and stand where they had been told.

As the pair turned to face the rest of the room, the mouths of both Sergeant Binks and

Sam dropped open. The walls of the room held a number of flaming torches, and standing on the floor against the walls were several large fire baskets burning ferociously. A large pentagram had been drawn on the floor in the centre of the room and around this stood at least fifty people all dressed in long black hooded cloaks. In the corner of the room stood two half naked men each loudly beating a kettledrum. The figures in the long-hooded cloaks swayed and chanted continuously to the rhythm of the drums.

Sergeant Binks turned to Sam,

"Bloody hell, what is this?"

"Exactly that, I think," Sam responded.

Suddenly the drums stopped. Another half-naked man, his skin painted blood red and wearing an over-sized mock ram's skull over his face, appeared theatrically out of a cloud of smoke. The chanting got louder until the masked figure raised his hand and then it too stopped.

"Who comes before me to join our Satanic Ritual Society, not to be confused with the Satanic Worship Club which only meets at weekends and not at all during July and August?" the masked man asked.

A naked man was led into the room and said,

"I, Jason Foster, wish to join your Satanic Ritual Society."

Sam turned to Sergeant Binks and whispered,

"That's him, that's the audiologist who has been hypnotising people to carry out the robberies."

"Steady now," Sergeant Binks replied and motioned Sam to be still.

"What do you bring to our society, Jason Foster?" the masked man asked.

"I bring jewels and money to further the cause of the society."

Jason then opened the metal box he was carrying to reveal the same.

"And how did you come by this?" the masked man asked.

"I hypnotise people to steal it on my behalf."

The masked man lifted his arms and, addressing the hooded figures present, asked,

"Do all my hobgoblins wish for Jason Foster to join us?"

"We do," was the united response.

"Excellent. Then Jason Foster you are indeed worthy. Are you prepared to be initiated into our society?"

"I am so prepared."

"Then bend over so that you may be hit upon the buttocks with a cricket bat while you sing the first four verses of Waltzing Matilda."

"Okay, that's it, I have seen enough," Sergeant Binks said to Sam and pulling his identification card from inside his jacket pocket he loudly announced to everyone present,

"This is the Police, nobody moves."

In the seconds which followed there was pandemonium, as face-covered hooded figures shouting various expletives raced this way and that out of the building as quickly as they could. Moments later the flickering light from the flaming torches and basket fires revealed all that remained of the satanic gathering, namely an almost unrecognisable chalk pentagram, a naked man wearing an expression of panic, a cricket bat and a metal box filled with money and jewellery. Sergeant Binks slowly walked over to a sheepish looking Jason Foster and said,

"Jason Foster I am arresting you for orchestrating the robberies of Hartigan's and Market Cross jewellery stores. You do not have to say anything. But it may harm your defence if you do not mention when questioned something which you later rely on in court. Anything you do say may be given in evidence."

7.

Despite his late and eventful night, Sam woke early. Over his breakfast cereal he reflected on his visit to the old mill and wondered how popular these satanic gatherings are. To the best of his knowledge, it is not something he had ever seen advertised. Is it reasonable to assume he thought, that if there is a god then there will therefore be a devil, who too moves in mysterious ways? Is it another one of these equal opportunities issues? And why all the costumes? Is that something which we have imported from Hollywood? Too many questions and not enough answers, he thought, while washing up his cereal bowl and coffee cup.

Before leaving for work Sam rang Simon and shared with him what had gone on the previous night. Also, Sergeant Binks' view that as far as the Police were concerned, as Jason Foster had confessed to his part in the robberies and as all of the stolen jewellery had been returned, they were not looking for anyone else in connection with the case. Simon was understandably very relieved but also, he told Sam, he was still inclined to contact the Sergeant to confess that it was he on the Market Cross cctv footage. He said doing so would make him feel much better, and enable him to get rid of the beret and false beard.

....

Sitting at his desk in his office Sam knew he still had his parents to face. He felt sure that despite his innocence they wouldn't be happy about his arrest and having to assist with his release. He foresaw yet another lecture questioning why he wanted to be a private investigator and why he didn't instead want to join the family business. He decided he might as well get it over with and go and visit them.

....

"Good morning, sir, please do come in," James the family butler said as he opened the front door of the family home. "I trust you are well."

"Actually James, I have come to face the music following my recent arrest. Are my parents about?"

"Lord and Lady Edgeware are presently in the drawing room, sir."

"Thank you, James, oh well here goes," Sam said rather despondently.

James coughed in a way which suggested he had something else to say.

"I do hope it was not inconvenient to you sir, but after you rang yesterday, I did not feel it would be conducive to share your circumstances with Lord Edgeware as you requested."

"I don't understand. So how was it that I was released?"

"Well sir, it just so happens that I am acquainted with the Deputy Chief Constable and it was I who made contact with him, and he I believe who arranged for your release."

"Acquainted? In what way?"

"If it is convenient to you sir, I would rather not discuss the details but suffice to say he once said, he owed me one."

"Well, I'll be blowed. Well done, James. Thank you."

"Thank you, sir."

"Well, I suppose as I am here, I might as well say hello to my parents," Sam said, much more positively.

"Lord and Lady Edgeware are currently taking tea with the Chief Constable."

"Just a quick hello then," Sam said, smiling broadly.

Sam entered the drawing room,

"Hello all, I was just passing and thought I would pop in to see how you both are."

"Oh, hello Brian."

"Bertram."

"That's right Bertram, isn't it," his mother said. "Have you met the Chief Constable? Your father and he are discussing how best to deal with some very annoying trespassers on our land."

"No, I don't think we have met before," said Sam, as he moved to shake the Chief Constable's hand. "Oh, I see you must have been doing a spot of decorating," he added, as he turned the Chief Constable's hand to reveal traces of blood-red paint under the fingernails.

The Casebook of Private Investigator Sam Sloane

A Toxic Spa

Stephen Towers

1.

On that particular morning it was an exceptionally red-faced private detective who opened his office door. Surprisingly, his secretary Barbara, who was sitting at her desk, was not on her mobile phone. She looked up and smiled.

"That looks painful," she said wincing and pointing to his face.

"It is," Sam replied.

"Did you have a nice holiday?" Barbara enquired.

"It was fine," Sam replied unconvincingly, and then looked reflectively into space and said, "A drunken guest got arrested for peeing into the hotel swimming pool......a hen party who were also staying at the hotel made loud and frequent use of a karaoke machine......a group of Sunderland football supporters got into a fight in the hotel restaurant and on the night before I left the drunken man who had peed in the swimming pool was released by police, returned to the hotel and I guess in an act of revenge, burnt the hotel down to the ground. Actually, it wasn't fine at all. I am pleased to be back. What is it with the English abroad?" Sam shook his head in bewilderment and went through into his office to be followed soon after by Barbara with a cup of coffee.

"Have you got anything to put on your sunburn?" she asked.

"I have put some calamine lotion on it, which I think has calmed it down a lot."

"Oh, it has, you can hardly notice it. In fact, I think it is really clever how you managed to get the outline of your sunglasses on your face. It looks quite natural."

"Any messages while I was gone?" Sam said, in an attempt to change the subject.

"Actually yes, just before you arrived a Mr Murphy rang. He said he would call to see you later this morning. He owns that posh spa on the edge of town," Barbara said, clearly impressed.

"I wonder what he wants," Sam replied.

"Maybe he will have something for your face." Barbara smiled sympathetically and left the room, which was probably a good idea.

Sam again reflected, what is it with the English abroad and why is it you don't seem to witness such embarrassing raucous behaviour from other nationalities? Although in fairness he thought, we have never invaded Poland or Ukraine and it wasn't us who first produced so called "reality tv shows." He took a sip of his coffee and wondered if instead of his recent holiday his money might have been better spent buying a coffee machine.

....

Sam sat at his desk examining his fingerprints, and his sunburnt skin through an inexpensive looking magnifying glass. He wasn't really sure what he was looking for and his mind soon drifted to the time when he got the magnifying glass. Somehow, it seemed that his name had been added to a mailing list and he had received an invitation to attend a convention for private detectives. Sam's initial reaction was to discard the invitation, more so when he read the small print advising that it cost £85 to attend. However, the more he thought about it the more he thought it may be a useful opportunity to check out the competition and it may even result in some business. So, he decided to go.

On the day of the conference, as first impressions go, Sam quickly began to regret his earlier decision. A skip overflowing with broken furniture, tarnished bathroom mirrors, and stained mattresses stood outside the entrance to the hotel which was the conference venue. Looking about at the unfashionable neighbourhood, Sam reluctantly pulled at the hotel's grubby entrance door and to his disappointment found that it opened. Wiping what he guessed was plaster dust from his hands, he entered a large but drab lobby which had a carpet with an apparent allergy to vacuum cleaners. A tall unshaven man, who gave every impression he had just got out of bed, stood behind a dust covered reception counter. He was reading what appeared to be a classic car magazine and scratching his chest through a dirty white shirt. He didn't look up when Sam entered. Sam gazed about and noticed a large handwritten sign sellotaped to a wall indicating that the conference was in the hotel's basement. Rather than break the concentration of the tall man, Sam crossed the lobby to the staircase. Going down the stairs he entered the basement through a badly scratched varnished door and was met by the distinct smell of dampness and a flickering, buzzing fluorescent light. But what shook him most was that everyone in the large room except Sam, appeared to be dressed in a Sherlock Holmes outfit. Sam had never seen so many deerstalker hats, tweed capes and gourd calabash pipes. It seemed that the convention was a celebration of Sir Arthur Conan Doyle's fictional private investigator. Sam uttered something unprintable under his breath, which was fortunate because he was warmly greeted by a very overweight looking Sherlock Holmes who was handing out name badges to all convention attendees. Recognising the unfortunate situation he found himself in, Sam had immediately pretended to receive an urgent call on his mobile phone and explained that unfortunately he had to leave right away. However, before he left, he was offered and graciously accepted a complimentary magnifying glass which was being given to all guests. Although Sam had been very tempted to deposit the item in the skip on his way out, he decided to keep it as it had effectively cost him £85.

Sam wondered what had happened to that hotel; if it still existed as such, or whether it had been converted like so many empty buildings into a betting shop. And what about all of those Sherlock Holmes wannabes, where are they now? His thinking was however interrupted by a knock on his office door. The door opened, it was Barbara.

"Mr Daniel Murphy is here to see you; shall I show him in?"

"Yes, please do," Sam replied, replacing his magnifying glass into his top desk drawer.

As instant initial impressions go Daniel Murphy was clearly the male equivalent of mutton dressed as lamb. In fact, he reminded Sam of a stereotypical porn star – not that Sam had seen a lot of pornographic movies. Daniel had slicked back blond hair and a blond horseshoe moustache, unnaturally brilliant white teeth, and large reflective sun glasses covered his eyes. He was wearing tan cowboy boots over white trousers which were so tight that he probably could never father children and a red silk shirt half unbuttoned to reveal a large gold medallion around his neck. Gold rings covered his fingers and a heavy gold bracelet hung limply from one of his wrists.

"Mr Sloane, how good of you to see me." Then as if distracted for a moment while looking about the office asked, "Are you in the middle of decorating?"

"Hello Daniel, nice to meet you. No, I am not decorating," Sam replied, a little perplexed by the question, and also now looking about his office.

The two men shook hands and staring at Sam's face Daniel asked,

"Are you unwell? If you don't mind me saying you look a little flushed."

"I am fine," Sam replied. "I have just been on holiday and caught a little too much sun."

"You should really put something on that. It looks rather painful."

"Tell me, Daniel, how may I help you?"

"Well, I do believe someone intends me harm."

"And what makes you say that?" Sam calmly enquired.

Daniel put his gold-coloured mobile phone and set of keys down on Sam's desk. Sam noticed the attached key ring which read, *"My other car is also a Porsche."* Sam wasn't surprised.

"This," he replied, and pulled a sheet of paper from the back pocket of his tight white trousers and passed it to Sam.

Sam opened the sheet of paper and found a message had been stuck to it using individual letters from various newspapers and magazines. The message read; *Your life is coming to an abrupt end.*

"Well, that's fairly succinct, I would say," Sam said, and added, "Lacks the personal touch but sticks to the point and gets the message across. Have you contacted the police?"

"No, I would rather not do that. You see I own a very successful company and am about to launch a big marketing campaign. Any adverse publicity could negatively impact on it."

"Don't you think this is serious?" Sam asked.

"Well, I don't know, it may well just be a practical joke. But at the same time, I would like it checked out even if just for my piece of mind."

"You have no idea who or why someone would send this?"

"No, not at all."

"When did you receive it?"

"Three days ago."

"And you have received nothing since?" Sam asked.

"Not until this morning when I got to my office and I found this on my desk. This is what prompted me to contact you." Daniel reached for his mobile phone and showed Sam a photo he had taken of a knife stabbed through a photograph of himself.

"I see. Well, as whoever did this was able to gain access to your office and knew when you were out, I would guess it may well be an inside job. How many staff do you employ?"

"Twenty-six."

"If you have no objection, I think the best way to approach this at least initially, is for me to visit your club under the pretence that I am interested in joining. Have you told anyone else about this note or the knife through the photograph?"

"Only my manager, Helen."

"Okay, I will need to have a chat with her."

"That won't be a problem, I can arrange that."

"Good, I will call around this afternoon at about three o clock if that is convenient to you."

"Thank you, Mr Sloane," and with that Daniel stood up from his chair took his keys and phone and left.

Sam looked about his office and thought, he is right you know; this place could do with a new coat of paint.

2.

Both the type of parked cars and the availability of valet car parking more than suggested to Sam that the spa was not generally frequented by your average person on the street. Unless that person happened to be an eccentric or secret millionaire, in which case strictly speaking, they would not be an average person on the street. He climbed the wide stone steps past the ornate potted olive trees and neatly manicured box-hedging and approached the spa's large entrance door, which unsurprisingly opened automatically and silently. Sam was welcomed by softly played classical music (Bach's Orchestral Suite No.3 in D if you were wondering) and stepped onto a highly polished mosaic floor.

"Good afternoon, sir, how may I help you?" a young man dressed in a smart grey suit enquired.

"Oh, hello," Sam replied. "I am thinking of joining your spa."

"Of course, you are sir. And may I say it would be an excellent choice if you decided to do so."

There was a period of silence between the two men during which the young man maintained a fixed smile at Sam, then Sam spoke again,

"How do I go about it?"

"You need to complete a written application, which you will find in our air-conditioned Registration Room, which is behind you and to your left. You will also find in there a selection of pens together with some refrigerated bottles of still and sparkling water should you require some refreshment. If there is anything on the application form which you are not sure of or wish further clarification on, there is a buzzer on the desk. Press that, and I will pop across."

"Thank you," Sam replied, and crossed the mosaic floor to the Registration Room which he discovered also contained several large potted palm plants, and a number of photographs of Daniel Murphy in conversation with television personalities and members of the royal family.

Sam sat down at the desk, picked up a pen and began completing one of the application forms. Sam found the questionnaire to be both extensive and eyebrow raising, and certainly not for the faint hearted. Nearing its completion, he decided to press the desk buzzer. Moments later the door to the room opened.

"You pressed the buzzer sir. How may I help?"

"Thank you. Just a couple of points. The two references you require. I see they must agree to pay the spa two hundred and fifty thousand pounds should I in any way, ever say anything negative about the spa."

"That is correct sir. That does of course include all taxes and any related legal fees."

"Also, should I join this spa, then I am not allowed to visit any other spa at home or abroad for the rest of my life?"

"That is correct sir. This is to prevent the transfer of any bacteria or other unwanted nasties from any of the other poorer quality spas to this one. We place great emphasis on the health and safety of our clients and therefore believe it to be of paramount importance to protect and maintain the high standards of cleanliness and hygiene which we set."

"I see," Sam replied, "and finally, and this may be covered partly by the earlier point, I believe it says should I in any way bring the name of the spa into disrepute then I am required to agree that any and all of my pets be turned into animal feed."

"That is correct sir. The spa does support a number of local charities in this way. It is our way of putting something back into the community." The young man smiled genially.

"Okay, so, what happens now?" Sam asked, passing the young man his completed application form.

"I will pass your application to the spa's manager, Ms Ferguson, who will review it and get back to you directly. In the meantime, if you would prefer, you may wish to avail yourself of one of our many healthy beverages in our comfortable Green Tea Lounge."

"Yes, I think I will do just that, thank you," Sam replied.

……………………..

Entering the spa's Green Tea Lounge a number of questions jumped into Sam's mind. I wonder who does their decorating? Is one of the people in here the potential murderer? And where do I sit?

Sam gazed upon a room where the walls were painted a brilliant white, as were the Romanesque columns which framed a small decorative pool with a central fountain. Lifesize stone statues of naked men and women who had it seemed mislaid their arms were dotted about the room. As were a number of large stone urns and exotic plants. To complete the feeling of warmth and relaxation, gold-coloured spot lights shone down from the sky-blue glass ceiling. Sam instinctively looked down at his shoes and as casually as he could tried to clean them on the back of his trouser legs.

"Good afternoon, sir, how may I help you?" a voice from behind him said.

Sam turned to see a young woman dressed in black trousers and waistcoat and a white blouse.

"Oh, hello there," Sam said, "I have just popped in for a drink while my application to join the spa is being considered, but there does not appear to be anywhere to sit."

"May I suggest one of our ergonomically heated loungers or possibly one of our Cleopatra loungers by the Tranquillity Pool?"

"I don't mean to be difficult but you don't happen to have a normal chair I could sit on do you?" Sam said.

"I am afraid not, sir. Not in the Green Tea Lounge. What can I get you to drink?"

"A cup of tea will be fine, thank you."

"What sort of tea would you like? We have Green Tea of course, Black Tea, Oolong Tea, Chamomile Tea, Ginger Tea, Peppermint Tea, Hibiscus Tea, and Fennel Tea."

"Mint Tea will be fine thank you," Sam said, then took off his raincoat and sat down rather awkwardly on an ergonomically heated lounger. Seeing little alternative he lay back, folded his raincoat and placed it on his lap. Looking about the room he had clearly caught the attention of many of the clients present, all of whom were dressed in white robes and some had white towels wrapped around their hair. Sam smiled at those whose eye he caught, some smiled back, others grimaced or turned away pretending not to have noticed him, or gave him a look which suggested they believed he had just quietly broken wind. It was the sort of look that reminded Sam of the expression he would get from his parents if he turned up at their home without an appointment.

Sam's mind turned to the task in hand. Who could have taken such a dislike to Daniel Murphy? Could it be one of the robed spa clients relaxing in the Green Tea room with Sam right now? Or was it one of the employees Sam had already met? Whoever it was, Sam thought, what was their motive? Was it that they had a very low tolerance toward men's jewellery and gold medallions in particular?

Sam nonchalantly looked about the room trying to determine if anyone present looked obviously guilty. Hoping for example, that he might catch one of them surreptitiously reading a *Murder for Beginners Handbook* or such like. Maybe, just maybe, of course, it may not be the first time the person concerned had done this. However, his train of thought was interrupted by the arrival of his mint tea.

"Are you alright Mr Sloane? If you don't mind me saying so you look rather hot. Your face is very red."

"Thank you, I have just returned from holiday and caught a little too much sun."

"We may have something for that in our medical room. Would you like me to check?"

"No, thank you for your concern, but I am fine."

"Well, if you are sure, you are okay. The spa's manager, Helen Ferguson, would like a word with you. If you would like to follow me, I will take you to her office."

3.

Sam knocked at the door marked "Manager" and a pleasant voice responded, "Come in."

Sam entered a small, bright and very tidy office. An attractive middle-aged woman stood up from behind her desk and shook Sam's hand.

"Good afternoon, Mr Sloane, I am Helen Ferguson, the spa's manager. Mr Murphy said you would be along this afternoon. Please take a seat," she said, pointing in the direction of a single polished metal framed chair in front of her desk.

"Now, how may I help you?" Helen asked.

"Thank you for making the time to see me. I understand Mr Murphy has appraised you of recent events and the possible threat on his life."

"Yes, indeed he has. I think at first he thought it was some sort of a joke, but this morning when he found that knife stuck through his photo, well I think that made him sit up and wonder if it could be more serious."

"Can you think of anyone who would do this?"

"No, I can't. However, I would say that I have only been here six months. Some of the staff have been here much longer than I and so may have a better idea."

"I understand the spa employs twenty-six people."

"That's right, although we have two vacancies at the moment."

"How did the vacancies come about?" Sam asked.

"One person left to resume her university course. As for the other, well it's not something you come across every day, he said he was leaving to become a polar explorer."

Sam made a facial expression which suggested he agreed that such a career move was not commonplace and then said,

"Do you have a big turnover in staff?"

"No, I wouldn't say any greater than any other like establishment," Helen replied reflectively and added, "We have a good relationship with the local employment agency, Lombard's, who seem to recognise the sort of person we are looking for."

"That's useful," Sam nodded. "Did Mr Murphy mention that I plan to act undercover, as it were and move around the place as if I were a spa member?"

"Yes, he did and therefore naturally I have signed off your application to join the spa. Despite you giving your references as Dr Hawley Crippen and Lucrezia Borgia."

"Sorry, my warped sense of humour," Sam smiled apologetically. Helen returned his smile.

"Your membership card will be waiting for you at reception. It is effective immediately."

"Thank you," Sam said, "It may be that I will need to speak with you again."

"Not a problem," Helen replied.

Closing the manager's office door behind him, Sam was surprised to see an old school chum of his.

"It's Biggles Braithwaite, isn't it?" Sam blurted.

"It certainly is. Bertie Edgeware, isn't it?" Biggles replied.

"It certainly is. What are you doing here?" Sam asked.

"I work here. Started a few months ago."

………………..

"Biggles" had been christened William Wilberforce Braithwaite after his Great Uncle Bill, who was a part time fortune hunter and full-time nutter. Great Uncle Bill was reputed to have been killed while demonstrating to a group of engrossed pygmies that a man-eating lion will not attack you if you stand on one leg and balance a brussels sprout on your head. If he was correct (it is not known if his theory has been tested since) it seems he must have used the wrong variety of sprout on that particular occasion.

While Sam's former classmate was neither a fortune hunter nor a complete nutter, at school he was always ready to have a go and would try most things (except worm eating) and it was because of this that he was nicknamed Biggles by his school chums. Hiis enthusiasm knew no bounds. Whenever a volunteer was called for, whether it was performing the duties of milk monitor or acting as the moving target in archery practice, to the relieved appreciation of the other students, Bill's arm would shoot up in the air with calls of "me sir, pick me sir, please sir." The Physics Master took it particularly badly when the time came for Bill to leave the school as he lost his test pilot for his jet pack invention and nuclear-powered rocket bike.

………………..

"I didn't know you were interested in health and fitness," Sam said.

"I'm not, well not in particular."

"So why are you working here?"

"Money Bertie. I am broke and I need the money."

"But I thought your parents had more money than Microsoft?"

"They do, but they have cut me off without a penny."

"I don't understand. Why would they do such a thing?"

"Because I refused to marry the daughter of Lord and Lady Bastock."

"I don't think I know her," Sam replied.

"Trust me, you would remember if you had met Morag. She has the personality of a rice cake and the figure of an elephant seal. She thinks belching is a form of social interaction. Honestly Bertie, she sounds like a stegosaurus bellowing across the steaming gaseous swamps of primeval earth."

"Not your type then?"

"No, and besides, I am engaged to another," Biggles announced rather proudly.

"Anyone I know?" Sam asked.

"I don't suppose so. Her name is Suzanne. Oh, Bertie she is witty, kind, thoughtful and really attractive," Biggles said excitedly. "I finish my shift in half an hour and I am meeting her in a café not far from here. Would you like to come along and meet her?"

"I would like that very much," Sam replied.

"By the way, what are you doing here? I didn't know you were a member."

"I will tell you all about it on our way to meet your fiancée."

....

Entering the coffee shop, Sam was much relieved to see that a defibrator had been hung on the wall. After Sam had shared in absolute confidence with his old friend that he was not only operating in the capacity of a private investigator at the spa, but also acting under the assumed name of Sam Sloane, Biggles appeared to be on the verge of exploding with excitement.

"Wow, this is great Bertie, I mean Sam. I have always wanted to do something like that. Do you carry a gun? Do you need a partner? Even just on a temporary basis. I could pack my job in. I am sure Suzanne would soon get me another one. Do you wear a bullet-proof vest. I thought I had one of those once but it didn't work. Do you want to see my scar? I have so many questions. Maybe I should go to the toilet first? No, I will go later. Sorry, enough for now, let me introduce you to Suzanne."

Thankfully Biggles took a deep breath and the two men walked over to a small table where a woman sat alone reading a book. She looked up as they approached.

"Bill, what is it? I don't think I have seen you this excited since that day you realised the engagement ring I said I liked was half price in the sale."

"It's just the sight of seeing you that sends my heart racing," Bill replied smoothly.

Then Bill turned to Sam,

"Sam this is my fiancée, Suzanne."

"Very nice to meet you," Sam said. "Bill has told me all about your whirlwind romance, how you met in this coffee shop and how you swept him off his feet."

Bill and Suzanne looked at each other and smiled. Sam's phone rang and taking it from his jacket pocket he saw it was his secretary, Barbara.

"Excuse me, but I need to take this. Nice to meet you, Suzanne. Probably see you tomorrow, Bill. Bye."

And with that Sam left the coffee shop.

"Hello Barbara."

"Who is this?"

"It's me Sam, you rang me remember."

"Oh yes, hello Mr Sloane, I was wondering if I could take Friday off as holiday?"

"Well, I think you may have already used up all of your holiday entitlement this year."

"Could I bring some forward from next year?"

"Holiday leave is not really designed to work that way," Sam replied.

"What if I make up the time and work until 3.00am Friday morning?"

"No, I don't believe we will get many callers or visitors at that time of night."

"What about a day sick?"

"Do you feel ill?"

"Not at the moment, but I could by Friday."

"What is so urgent that you need to take the day off?"

"Well, I thought I might have my nails done."

"That's it?" Sam said in an astonished voice.

"That's what?" Barbara replied.

"Never mind. Just take the day off before I die of old age."

"Oh, thank you Mr Sloane that is very kind of you. Not for a moment did I think you would agree to it. And I hope you don't die of old age or anything else for that matter.

Although I suppose we all die at some point. Well, I hope you don't die any sooner than you should. Not that you should die if you know what I mean. But of course, nobody lives forever. Although I am not sure about Peter Pan. By the way, Daniel Murphy rang, he was wondering how you were getting on."

"Ring him back and tell him I will call in and see him tomorrow."

"Do you have his number?"

"Not on me, no. You could look it up," Sam said rather exasperated.

"That's a good idea," Barbara replied. "Okay I will see you in the morning, bye."

"Actually I won't…." but the connection had gone.

4.

The following day, in accordance with the advice he had been given when he had collected his spa membership card, Sam arrived at the spa thirty minutes early for his first scheduled treatment, a sauna. Thankfully, having only just returned from holiday he had been able to readily find his swimming shorts. Unfortunately these were just too big to squeeze into his coat pocket, so he carried them in a worn sports bag he'd had at university. He normally used the bag to store odd socks which his washing machine regularly generated on wash days. Unlike some of the other spa clients he had observed the day previous, Sam was comfortable with a less pretentious image.

Climbing the spa's steps Sam heard a distinct "psst" which made him look around.

"Good morning, Bill, are you well?" Sam said and smiled.

"What do you think of Suzanne?"

"She seems very nice. Sorry I had to dash off as I did."

"Not a problem. Don't forget if you need anything, I am your man," Bill replied and winked, and then dashed off with several cardboard boxes he was carrying.

Sam presented his pristine membership card to the young woman standing behind the reception desk.

"Oh, I see you are a new member, Mr Sloane. Welcome to the spa, my name is Vicky."

"Good morning, Vicky, nice to meet you. Have you worked here long?"

"About a year now."

"Nice place to work, is it?"

"Much better than the place I used to work. I used to work in a slaughter house sweeping up the entrails of the dead animals."

"That doesn't sound very pleasant," Sam said, pulling a face.

"That wasn't the worse of it. At the end of each day, we had to collect and bag up all the eye balls from the carcasses. And sometimes you had to prize them out of the animal's skull with a tea spoon."

"Sounds disgusting," Sam said, feeling himself retching.

"If that wasn't bad enough…."

Sam interrupted,

"Is that the time. Sorry Vicky but I would love to stand here and chat with you but I have a sauna booked."

"Not a problem. Here is your spa robe and slippers. Go through that door on your right and follow the signs. Hopefully I will catch you later. Bye for now."

………………..

Sam entered a small room with several changing cubicles. A very large man wearing baggy white trousers, brown sandals and a white t shirt which hung over his ample stomach rather like a lampshade, greeted him.

"Good morning, sir, you must be Mr Sloane. My name is Jim. "Big Jim" some people call me, for some reason. I look after the sauna and the steam room here at the spa. Can I ask, have you used a sauna before?"

"Yes, although it was some years ago now," Sam replied.

"You can't be too careful with them, used the wrong way they can be dangerous. Some people don't realise how hot they can get. Did you know the human body is almost sixty per cent water? I don't know how many times I have returned from my lunch to find just a pool of blubber on the floor of this sauna. "Are you feeling alright?" I would ask the customer but they had just melted away. Personally, I don't think saunas get that hot. Do you know a good friend of mine was crossing the Sahara Desert on a camel, now he told me that it got so hot that his camel burst into flames and he had to walk the rest of the way. Ruined a perfectly good pair of shoes he said. Yet when he came here to use this sauna, he reckoned that it was hotter than the desert. Just goes to show you that you can never tell."

"Do you use the sauna or steam room yourself?" Sam asked.

"Me? No way. You wouldn't get me into one of those coffins. I suffer from claustrophobia. I like open spaces. I always wanted to be a jockey."

"Just grew too tall, did you?" Sam asked trying to be tactful but still rather surprised by Jim's response.

"No, my hair wasn't curly enough."

"Sorry?" Sam replied, obviously confused.

"My hair wasn't curly enough. You have to have curly hair if you want to be a jockey. I tried all sorts of treatments recommended by all the top consultants. From massaging the fresh contents of a baby's nappy into my scalp to burning all my hair off with a kitchen blow torch. Nothing worked.

"So, what is it like working at the spa?" Sam asked trying to move the conversation topic on.

"Fine, I guess. I spend all my money on hairdressing and toupee magazines."

....

Sam's time in the sauna reflecting on jockey's hairstyles passed quickly. Then after a chilled blueberry smoothie, Sam made his way to the spa's jacuzzi suite where he was met by a tall, slim, middle-aged woman.

"Hello Sam, I understand you are new here. My name is Belinda. Welcome to our Hydrotherapy and Jacuzzi Suite. If you have any questions, anything at all, please do not hesitate to ask."

Like Jim, Belinda was dressed in white trousers, a rather tight fitted white t shirt and brown sandals.

"Have you used a jacuzzi before, Sam?"

"Not in some time."

"Well, I will just briefly run through the controls before you get in. We don't want any accidents, do we?" Belinda said and laughed.

After a short explanation Sam got into the bath and switched on the jets.

"Now, it's not a good idea to put oils or salts into a jacuzzi as it can clog the filters and damage the purification system, so I tend to light a number of aromatic candles just to get us in the mood," Belinda said.

"In the mood?" Sam asked quizzically.

"Just a figure of speech. You don't mind do you Sam?"

"No, not at all."

"Has anyone mentioned what lovely eyes you have?"

"Well now that you mention it, no."

"Are you married Sam?"

"No, I am not."

"Do you have a steady partner?"

"Not at the moment, no."

"What do you think of these candles?"

"Er, they are very nice."

"They are aren't they," Belinda said. "Really makes you want to do something you may regret. Don't you think?"

"Well...."

"I often enjoy doing things I sometimes regret. Did I mention I am not married either."

"No, you didn't. Tell me, have you worked here long?" Sam asked.

"A while, you sure that water isn't too hot? I must say it looks very inviting."

"What is Mr Murphy like to work for?"

"He is okay."

"Does he have any enemies that you are aware of?"

"What?" Belinda asked, clearly surprised at the question. "No, not that I know of, although of course there has always been questions about the death of his wife and how he got the money for this place."

"Really? What exactly do you mean?"

Just at that moment Belinda's mobile phone rang. She answered it.

"Yes, I see, well I am with a spa customer at the moment. Very well, I will be right there." She turned back to Sam. "I am sorry I must go, don't forget to pull the plug and blow the candles out when you leave.

"Of course. Thank you. Bye."

....

Sam's final appointment of the morning was for a back, neck and shoulders massage in treatment room four. When Sam got there, he found the door to the room slightly ajar, he pushed at it and as he did so a voice from within the room said, "come in." Sam entered to see a tall man with biceps the size of a small village in East Sussex. He was lifting a pair of large dumbbells and around his thick neck was hung a car engine.

"Sam Sloane, I presume," the tall man said, smiling and putting his exercise weights and the engine down on a nearby bench which buckled under the strain.

"That's right."

"My name is Dave," the man replied and shook Sam's hand with a vice-like grip.

"Do you work out, Sam?"

"Erm, not as often as I should," Sam replied a little sheepishly.

"You should, we need to be ready for when they arrive, which they will."

"Most definitely…. Who are they by the way?"

"The Russians of course. I think it is a matter of time before they invade this country. Now hang your robe over there if you would and lie face down on the massage table."

Sam did as he had been instructed and Dave began the massage treatment.

"You see, Sam, the Russians. are a paranoid race, they just can't help themselves. The simple fact of the matter is you can't trust a Russian. They always deny it of course but if you ask me, they are always out to cause trouble. Did you know in the last twenty years alone they have been involved in seven wars. If you ask me, they have already infiltrated our society. Whenever something goes wrong, whether it's your coffee machine stopped working, a flat tyre on your car, or your hair beginning to turn grey, ask yourself, "Is there a Russian about?" You bet your life there is."

"Why is it you think they want to invade England?" Sam asked.

"Well, it's obvious isn't it, Stonehenge. It's older than the pyramids, nobody seems to know conclusively why it was built, who built it or how it was built. Being such a suspicious lot, the Russians obviously think it is some sort of secret doomsday weapon and they want it. Well, they can't have it. It's ours and we are keeping it."

"I see," Sam said unconvincingly. "Changing the subject completely for a moment, what do you know about Mr Murphy's wife?"

"Not a thing. She is not Russian, is she?"

It was nearing lunchtime when Sam's massage was done and he thought he would see if Daniel Murphy was free.

5.

Sam knocked at the polished oak office door.

"Come in," a man's voice replied; he sounded preoccupied. Opening the door Sam found Daniel Murphy sitting at a large desk staring at a piece of paper. He looked up as Sam entered the room. "Oh, Sam thank goodness it is you. I have been out all morning and just returned to my office to find this." Daniel handed Sam the piece of paper he had been staring at. Like the earlier message Daniel had received it was written using cut out letters from a newspaper. It read,

You know what you did. Now it is time for you to pay. At precisely 3.30pm today leave £10,000 in a Sainsburys carrier bag in the waste bin outside the Roasted Bean café. This buys you 24 hours. No Police or funny business or you will regret it.

"What is it this person believes you have done?" Sam asked.

"I don't know. I really don't know. What do you think I should do Sam?"

"Well, I know the note says no Police, but…"

"No, no Police," Daniel stressed.

"Well, the final decision is of course yours. I know the café referred to; it is opposite the entrance to the park. If you can lay your hands on £10,000, I could be at the park and photograph the blackmailer when he or she collects the money. I am still of the view that this is an inside job and therefore I am certain you will be able to identify the person concerned from the photograph."

"At least paying up may buy you some extra time to discover who this person is," Daniel said hopefully. "Have you discovered anything yet at the spa?"

"A few things to think about certainly, but nothing conclusive as yet I am afraid regarding your case. If you don't mind me asking Daniel, are you married?"

"Unfortunately, no longer. My wife died in a boating accident several years ago. Why do you ask?"

"I am just trying to establish a complete picture. Nothing more," Sam said, and smiled.

Glancing at his watch Daniel stood up and announced,

"I had better get off to the bank in case there are any problems in me withdrawing this amount of money. There shouldn't be, they know me well."

"Keep me advised how you are getting on," Sam said.

"I will," Daniel said, then picked up his car keys and mobile phone and left.

Sam sat down on the corner of the large desk and looked about the room. A tall bookcase stood against one wall and had numerous framed photographs on it. Next to this was a filing cabinet and on another wall was a large-screen tv. Sam studied the latest note, he kept turning the phrase "you know what you did" over in his mind. Was Daniel keeping something from him? He seemed anxious not to involve the Police. Wouldn't you want to if your life was being threatened? If not, why not? What had Daniel done that he was in denial of? And what is the attraction of "man jewellery" – are you allowed to say that anymore or is it now classed as sexual harassment? Suddenly Sam was distracted by a person he saw through the large office window who appeared to be tending the gardens of the spa. Could he have seen something? Sam decided to find out.

....

"Excuse me, mate," Sam said as he made his way through the neatly terraced garden area.

"What makes you think I am a man?" the gardener replied in an affronted tone.

"Well, I saw you through the office window and assumed by the way you are dressed...."

"Are you saying members of the female gender can't dress like this?"

"Well, no, I just thought the way you dressed, your stature...."

"What, are you saying all females must be super models?"

"Well, no, I just guessed by the way you dressed, your stature, your physical activity......"

"Are you saying persons of the female gender are incapable of physical activity?"

"You have a bloody beard," Sam said loudly.

"Oh yea, well there is that. But before we go any further, I just want to make the point that one of the problems inherent within society today is that people just jump to conclusions. People have rights, and feelings too. Just because I am a man does not mean that I do not have the right to be a woman. For all you know I might be more comfortable being referred to as Lolita rather than Fred and wearing a cheeky cocktail dress with stiletto heels and a matching clutch bag for work – although I do recognise the practical problems that may bring. But did you attempt to find out? No. So, what can I do for you?"

"Forget it," Sam said and returned to the spa.

The time was approaching 2.30pm when Sam's mobile phone rang.

"Hello Sam, it's Daniel. I have the money. So, I will wrap it in a Sainsbury's bag and deposit it in the bin at 3.30 as instructed."

"Fine. I will make my way to a suitable place to take the photograph of our blackmailer. And I will get back to you and let you know how I get on."

....

Despite being delayed by a middle-aged woman asking to borrow the underwear he was wearing, Sam made it to the park in time to see Daniel deposit the £10,000 into the waste paper bin.

In order to get a clear photograph Sam squeezed himself between an overgrown rhododendron bush and the park's boundary railing. It wasn't easy as he tried to avoid the unwanted remains of a doner kebab and the numerous McDonalds drink cartons and wrappers which the wind had blown under the shrub. Each passing minute seemed like ten as

Sam waited silently and patiently for the person to take the orange carrier bag from the waste bin. He held his mobile phone camera at the ready to get that all important shot. Suddenly and unexpectedly a bus came to a halt, obscuring the waste bin from Sam's view. He couldn't believe his bad luck and instinctively knew this was the moment the blackmailer had been waiting for. Sam struggled to get out from behind the large bush and ripped the sleeve of his raincoat as he did so. By the time he managed to cross the road and under the watchful eyes of the surprised people sitting in the Roasted Bean café, checked the waste bin, he found the carrier bag had gone. Not only that but looking down Sam also realised that while standing next to the rhododendron he had inadvertently stood in some dog muck.

Sam rang Daniel, who had been anxiously awaiting his call, and explained what had happened. Sam also took the opportunity to ask for a list of any and all spa employees who had been absent from work that afternoon.

"Not a problem," Daniel replied, "I will ask Helen as soon as she comes in tomorrow.

She has been out this afternoon." There was a pause.

"Hello," Sam said.

"Oh, sorry Sam, I was just thinking," Daniel said in a thoughtful voice. "You don't think it could be Helen, do you?"

"Well, let's not jump to any conclusions," Sam replied. "If you can get me that list and I will see you in the morning."

Sam returned to the park to find a quiet spot where, as casually as possible, he could try and wipe the dog muck from his shoe.

6.

The following morning Sam lay in bed. He was doing his best to ignore the loud knocking on his front door. He knew who it was. It was his neighbour Brendan. He knocked at this time most mornings with the same two questions. Brendan wanted to know whether Sam thought the world might end today, in which case he wouldn't bother hanging out his washing but would return his library book, and whether Sam knew anything about electrical wiring. The latter was the result of a recent incident when Brendan had fitted a homemade camera sensor to his front door, but due to a miscalculation of some sort had managed to vaporise a passing neighbourhood cat. (What neither Brendan nor Sam appreciated was that had the cat not been inadvertently vaporised, it would in the next moment have been chased by a stray dog across a busy road, causing a tanker of radioactive waste to swerve and crash and lay waste to a large area for two million years).

Once he was convinced the knocking had stopped, Sam got out of bed, washed, dressed and had some breakfast. Then having checked his neighbour wasn't anywhere to be seen outside, he left for the spa.

Despite the relatively early hour the spa car park was already busy. Sam saw his school mate Biggles parking customers cars by means of speedy handbrake turns. The space reserved for Daniel Murphy was occupied by a bright yellow Porsche. Sam crossed the spa's entrance lobby, smiling at Vicky who was behind the reception desk as he did so. At first glance Vicky appeared to be juggling several sheep's eye balls. Sam didn't look back to check but made his way to Daniel's office.

"Morning, Sam," Daniel said with a slight smile.

"Hello, Daniel, how are you today?"

"Well, so far so good. At least I am still here."

"Got to be positive," Sam said.

"Helen is in and I have asked her to prepare that list you requested of staff who were absent yesterday afternoon."

"Good, I will go and see her about that. Have you heard anything further since the cash drop off?"

"Nothing."

"Let me know straight away if you hear anything. Otherwise, I will be back to see you mid-afternoon."

....

"Good morning, Helen, I understand you have a list of absentee staff for me."

"Well, it's not much of a list. The only absent staff member yesterday afternoon was Diane, who is heavily pregnant and was attending a pre-natal appointment at the local hospital."

"Mmm, I see," Sam said looking at the short list. "If you don't mind me asking, where were you yesterday afternoon?"

"I was at the Lombard Employment Agency shortlisting for those two vacant posts I mentioned to you when we first met."

"Ah yes, would you let me have the contact details of those two previous members of staff please."

"Not a problem. Unfortunately, I don't appear to have a mobile phone contact for either of them, but I do have the home address for Michael Hammond; and Marjorie Wilberforce was going to attend Edinburgh University. I believe she said she was to study Classics."

"Thank you I will follow those up."

"Before you go," Helen said in a very serious tone, "am I a suspect?"

"At the moment everyone is a suspect," Sam replied with a wry smile. He had always wanted to say that.

………………..

Sam rang the doorbell of an unremarkable modern terraced house. It looked exactly the same as so many modern houses,

Sam thought. The only variation appeared to be the colour of the front door and the type of window blinds the occupier installed. The door was opened by a short rotund man wearing a blue woollen dressing gown.

"Can I help you?" the man asked politely.

"Are you Michael Hammond?"

"I am indeed."

"My name is Sam Sloane. I have been engaged by Daniel Murphy. I believe you know him."

"Yes, he owns the spa where I used to work. Would you like to come in?"

Sam was shown into a small living room with beige wooden louvre blinds.

"Is anything wrong?" Michael asked.

"Do you mind if I ask you where you were yesterday afternoon between three and four o clock?"

"Not at all. I was visiting my mother at the Bay View Nursing Home."

"Oh yes, I think I know it," Sam replied.

"And before that I was at the Discovery Centre checking out the space exploration exhibition."

"Sounds interesting, but I have been given to understand that you left your employment at the spa to become a polar explorer?"

"I did, I was convinced that was what I wanted to do. I got all the gear. Come through here I will show you."

Sam was shown into a room packed from floor to ceiling with skis, sleeping bags, snow shovels, a tent, thermal clothing, an amphibious sled, ropes of various sizes and colours, a medical kit, a dog harness, goggles, ice picks, insulated gloves, polar boots, ski poles, stoves and toilet paper.

"Wow," Sam said, "I had no idea you required so much equipment."

"Oh yes," Michael replied, "you have to be prepared for every eventuality. I even sponsored a penguin, called Joseph."

"I must say it all looks very impressive."

"Do you know anyone who may want to buy it?" Michael asked in a hopeful voice.

"Well, not off the top of my head you understand, but I will bear it in mind. So, what now for you if you have decided not to be a polar explorer?"

"Space is the place for me. I have written to NASA and expect to hear back from them at any time. In fact, when I saw you at the door, I thought you may be from them. I have been in training."

"What sort of training?" Sam asked.

"Follow me," Michael said excitedly.

Sam and Michael went upstairs and over the top of his moon-rocket patterned cotton pyjamas Michael pulled on protective elbow and knee pads, a thick pair of gloves and a motorbike crash helmet. Then, motioning Sam to stand back, Michael threw himself down the stairs.

"What are you training for when you do that?" a very surprised Sam asked.

"Re-entry to the Earth's atmosphere. Apparently, it can be very bumpy," a dazed Michael replied.

"Well, I wish you every success with your training and your NASA application. I really must go now. Thank you for the demonstration and good luck selling your polar gear."

"Would you like to see me fall off the roof?" Michael asked eagerly as Sam made his way down the short garden path.

"Another time, maybe," Sam said, and waved goodbye.

....

The Lombard Employment Agency was located just off the town's high street, sandwiched between a betting shop and a long-established hairdresser – the sort of hairdressers which exuded a strong ammonia smell when you passed by. Opening the main entrance door to the agency, Sam was surprised to see Bill's fiancée sitting at the reception desk.

"Hello Suzanne, I didn't realise you worked here."

"Yes, I have been working here part time for about six months now. What are you doing here?"

"I understand that Helen Ferguson from the health spa was here yesterday. As I was passing, she asked me to call in and see if she left any papers here."

"Yes, Helen was here all yesterday afternoon. I will check to see if she left anything. I didn't realise you knew Helen. I thought it was you I saw at the spa earlier when I dropped Bill off, as I sometimes do."

Suzanne made a telephone call and confirmed Helen had not left any papers that anyone knew of.

"Thanks for checking," Sam said. "Sadly, I must dash. Nice to meet you again. Bye for now," and Sam quickly made his exit.

Unfortunately, it was clear to Sam that his investigations were not going well. He needed time to think and he also needed to use a toilet. He called into the *Badger and Carrot* pub which was nearby. There he found a quiet corner and over a pint of local beer and a packet of crisps he made some phone calls.

....

It was just after 2.30pm when Sam returned to the spa. There he found Daniel staring out of his office window.

"Is that a cocktail dress Fred is wearing?" Daniel asked.

"Looks like it," Sam replied.

"Anyway," Daniel said turning to face Sam, "have you been able to make any progress?"

"Not yet. Have you heard anything?"

"Not a thing."

Sam went through what he had done and how he had checked and confirmed the reasons for absence of Helen and Diane and how the alibies of Michael Hammond and Marjorie Wilberforce had also stood up to test. Then suddenly there was a loud knock on Daniel's office door. It was Bill.

"Mr Murphy, you had better come quick, your car is on fire."

Sam looked at his watch; it was 3.30pm. Exactly 24 hours, he thought.

7.

As far as the firefighters were concerned, extinguishing the car fire was just another day in their life. As far as Daniel was concerned, it was a rather more notable event. Before his eyes his precious bright yellow Porsche had been transformed into a mound of bubbling foam.

It took about an hour for the firemen to tidy up their equipment and for the spa's customers to get their cars out of the car park. Sam and Daniel went back inside the building and made their way back to Daniel's office. Entering the room and then closing the oak office door, Daniel turned to Sam and said,

"So, where do we go from here?"

"Well…" Sam said but was immediately interrupted by another voice.

"I will tell you where you go," and the high-backed leather desk chair which had been facing the wall swung around.

"Suzanne!" Sam exclaimed in astonishment.

"Who is this? And what are you doing sitting in my chair?"

"You don't recognise me, do you Daniel?"

"No, I do not."

"I am your wife. The person you left to drown."

"Lola? But I didn't leave you to drown, and you look so very different."

"Yes, I do, don't I? That is because I have lost four stone, had some facial cosmetic surgery and changed the colour of my hair."

"Wow, you look really good."

"And you left me to drown. Now I am going to ruin you."

"But I didn't leave you to drown. As soon as I got to shore, I contacted the police who also searched. I hired a boat and offered a reward to encourage people to help me find you. I still have all of the emails I sent to the island's governor asking for assistance. You were nowhere to be found."

"Really?" Lola said, rather less accusingly.

"Yes, I have missed you so much. Look at my office bookshelves, they are covered in photos of you."

"Was I really that fat?" Lola said glancing at the photographs.

"What happened to you that day?" Daniel asked.

"I don't know exactly. I have assumed I must have somehow been knocked unconscious when I fell from our boat. When I came to, I found myself on a small island occupied by a hippy commune. I had lost my memory. It only came back about a year ago. I managed to return to this country where I saw your picture in a local paper. You were being given some business award. I guessed you had spent my life insurance on this place, that ridiculous man jewellery and a mid-life crisis car. That's when I decided to exact my revenge."

"You were going to kill me!"

"I wasn't going to kill you, you idiot. I thought it was so unfair that you appeared to be enjoying this lifestyle. I also thought you must have found someone else."

"There is nobody else. Oh, how I have missed you."

Sam interrupted,

"I don't believe there is anything else for me to do here so I think it is probably a good time for me to go."

Neither Daniel nor Lola answered.

………………..

Leaving the spa Sam saw Bill.

"Hello Sam," Bill said, "You haven't seen Suzanne, have you? I see her car is parked over the road."

"Yes, I have. Do you fancy a pint? I know a good pub down the road. I don't think Suzanne will mind."

Over a pint of local beer Sam and Bill enjoyed a reminisce about their school days. Then, after a couple more pints, Sam told Bill that Suzanne was in fact Lola and she was already married and basically had used Bill to get to Daniel.

"I think I need a fresh start, something new, miles from here," Bill said with a slurred voice.

"Have you ever thought of going on a Polar expedition? I know where there is a lot of gear going cheap," Sam replied.

Stephen Towers

ABOUT THE AUTHOR

Born in Northumberland in 1958, Steve has lived most of his life in North Yorkshire with his wife Jude.

Since his retirement from full-time work, Steve has written several books. The royalties from which are all donated to charity.

Other books written by Steve:

Travels in Absurd Times

Experiences and Observations of a non-celebrity

Mystery Shopping Everyday life

Sam Sloane Private Investigator

The return of Private Investigator Sam Sloane.

Printed in Great Britain
by Amazon